Wild Fading Laughter
By
Jack Judson

To my two favorite Rays:
Raymond & Etta Rae
I love you both.

"Love everyone and tell the truth." — *Neem Karoli Baba*

Part One

∞

one

A guy walks into a bar. My bar—I'm the owner of the joint. It's dark and loud and crowded. But I notice this guy right away. Looks like a movie villain—burly, shaved head, scarred face, black turtle neck, leather jacket. He elbows his way through the crowd and comes straight at me. Talks with a Russian accent. Big Bad Boris, I call him. He's drunk and wants a Long Island Iced Tea. I tell him we don't serve those here. But he pounds on the bar and insists. And I don't want to deal, so I tell him I'll make him one of my super famous magic lemonades—stronger than a Long Island, strongest drink he's ever had—but it will cost him a hundred bucks. A Bridge and Tunnel, I call it. He says he'd love one, and I laugh, because I'm assuming he's messing with me. But then he throws a wad of cash on the bar. And money is money, so I make him one. Put a shot of every liquor we got into a shaker, mix it with lemon juice and sugar, and pour it into this gigantic antique chalice we keep as a prop behind the bar. I top it off with every type of garnish, lace the rim with Absinthe, and light the whole thing on fire. It's a spectacular flaming cesspool.

Big Bad Boris loves it. He chugs the first one, then orders another—and another and another. Chugs them all. Then starts mouthing off. But I've got no idea what he's talking about. I'm surprised he can even stand up. He's slurring his words and waving his hands around like an orchestra conductor. I'm not even sure whether he's speaking English or Russian. But I nod my head and smile, because I'm a bartender—it's my job.

Boris reaches out and grabs my arm. And I know immediately, this isn't going to end well. He leans into me, jabs his finger in my face, and yells, "You know what? You've got ferocity. That's what I love about Americans, their ferocity. And you've got it, boychik! The American Ferocity. You got it! You! Got! It!"

"Umm…thanks?" I say, and back away.

Boris gulps the last of his drink. "But don't lose it," he says squinting at me and lowering his voice, "You hear me, boychik? Don't lose it. Don't get soft or you'll lose it. Your American Ferocity!" Then he leans back and smashes the chalice onto the floor.

"Hey!" I yell. Boris throws a punch at me, but whiffs. I jump over the bar and shove him. He stumbles into the crowd and falls to the floor. While he's down and struggling to get up, I swipe his wad of cash off the bar and stick it in my pocket—I'll consider it a tip.

Boris puts up a good fight as I drag him through the crowd. Gets all up in my face. We scuffle—pushing, shoving, and cursing back-and-forth. Same old riffraff drill. He's way bigger than me and much stronger, but he's wicked drunk, so I'm able to keep him off-balance and get him out the door, but not without knocking him into a girl outside. He falls face first on the pavement. But I'm more concerned about the girl. I turn to her and apologize, make sure she's okay—offer her and her friends a bottle of champagne. "On the house," I say. But wouldn't you know it, while I'm distracted, Big Bad Boris gets up, grabs me, turns me, and sucker-punches me right in the mouth. I drop. Everything goes black.

I lost the American Ferocity.

∞

two

My name is Victor Carroll, and for as long as I can remember I've wanted to be famous. I know that's a superficial and selfish thing to say—especially as a first impression, especially now as I look back on this idea—on this part of the story—with embarrassment. But it's the truth: money, power, fame—I wanted it all. To be an icon. The Red Sea parting before me when I walked into a room. Millions of fans screaming out my name in adulation. Every wish and desire fulfilled with the snap of my fingers. Bluntly—I wanted to be a god. I imagine lots of people have this dream at some point—probably almost everyone—I bet you've had this fantasy too. Except for me, it was an obsession—a parasite—my body the host for this deep, aching, pulse living inside me. An Ego Demon. And look—I know this admission doesn't exactly paint me rose-colored—but after all I've been through—I owe it to you—and to myself—to be honest—or at least to try anyways. Because I have come to the conclusion that life is about trying to love everyone and tell the truth. But it wasn't always that way. And this is that story.

It started out simple enough. When I was little and couldn't fall asleep during naptime at nursery school, the Catholic Nuns bribed me with candy to get me to be quiet and lay still. And something clicked: if I acted out—acted different from everyone else—I got special attention and special treats. Lesson learned. From there—I started looking for attention all over the place. Temper tantrums, class clown, delinquent. But also—obedient good-boy, model student, and overachiever. Yin and Yang. I adapted myself to the situation. Consummate diplomat or master manipulator? Both. As long as people were paying attention to me, I felt different—I mattered. That feeling of nothing inside, that sense of being a loser, a nobody, a living ghost, it all disappeared. I became special. I was special.

The constant Christ Rhetoric the nuns shoved down our throats over the course of twelve plus years in parochial school had something to do with it as well. "Jesus was thirty-three when he died. Think of all the things he accomplished. What will you have accomplished by then?" The holy spinsters used to remind us of this all the time. I think they intended this message to be inspirational—but for me, it just gave me a complex. That my life would be a failure unless I did the equivalent of providing salvation for all humankind by thirty-three. That's how it all got started. Well, that—and the rest of my childhood—but I'm going to leave that alone for now.

In my attempts to be famous, I tried music first. To be a rockstar. But I couldn't sing or play any instruments. My mom once told me I sang like a pig at slaughter. Music clearly wasn't going to work. And I'm not athletic—so sports got scratched fast too. And I certainly wasn't good looking enough to be an actor. And forget politics—I said I wanted to be liked, not universally hated. Wall Street seemed possible—on account of my smarts and social skills. And finance had its perks. Business folks aren't famous—but they sure are filthy rich. But I didn't have the drive for those hours. Instead, I focused on what I was best at: books and movies.

I spent my whole childhood—all my time—reading books and watching movies. I thought for a quick minute about being a writer. But come on—who becomes famous for being a writer nowadays? No one even reads anymore. To be honest—I'm not even sure why I'm writing this now—especially after all that's happened. Because of vanity and one last shot at fame perhaps? Because I'm trying to be a better person? Because I'm looking for forgiveness? Because the world can be cold and cruel and lonely, and certain books at certain times felt like hands reaching out from the pages and embracing me with love? Because maybe, just maybe, my silly story might do the same for someone else someday—might do it for you? Something like that.

With that said, early on, I was too afraid to write. I wasn't brave enough to tell a story that was important to me—to share my deepest hopes and fears with the high chance of having them go unread and unrecognized. Or mocked. I wanted to be famous, remember? So I focused all my attention on movies. They were the way to fame. I'd become a director. A famous one. Just like that—the most famous. Become a real Hollywood juggernaut—some kind of uber-auteur—the Jesus Christ of cinema. But it takes perseverance and talent and luck to make it in film. And I lacked all three. So just like a two-bit character from a mafia movie, I took the easy way out and settled on being a gangster—my scum pond version of one anyway. Look—I didn't set out to be a drug dealer—it just kind of happened. Let me explain.

I left home the day after my high school graduation. Said goodbye to my rotten past, packed a bag, and took the bus to New York City. I worked in restaurants, filled out some applications, took out loans I could never afford to pay back, and enrolled in an overpriced film school. Then I maxed out my credit to actually make a film. But it was terrible—a complete failure. Went into deeper debt—went broke. And then, like many other poor artists before me, I buried my dreams and started bartending full-time. And wouldn't you know it, I was good at it. Started working the high-end clubs and speakeasies. And with that came a certain kind of lifestyle. I became famous. Well, kind of—famous in my pathetic pocket of the universe. But for a while, that small pocket was just fine for me—booze, cash, and enough excitement to keep me satisfied. To give me the illusion of fame.

Now for some, the jump to being low-level drug dealer might seem like a leap, but it's really quite simple. Drugs were everywhere in the bars and clubs—always around and all centrally located in one place. And on most nights, I was in charge of that place. Why not capitalize on the opportunity? Location, location, location. Supply and demand. It was Econ101. Simple. That was my thinking anyways.

First, I met Bobby and Marco. Bobby was a rich Long Island trust fund kid with an architectural design degree and a desire to open a bar. The type of guy who considered fox hunting and midday lap dances at midtown strip clubs normal weekday activities. The type of guy who despite wearing a Rolex once attempted to microwave bacon on tin foil. As for Marco, what you need to understand most about him is this: he's a charmer—smooth and sexy. Marco is the type of guy who's got the pulse of the world in his palm. When he walks into the room, all eyes turn towards him. When he talks to you, and holds your gaze, all else vanishes. That type of guy—a rare breed.

Marco also had the most enviable of all intangibles—everyone he met fell in love with him. He was pure ecstasy. He preferred men, but enjoyed women too, because "I like beautiful things," he used to say. He was pretty much the guy that every adolescent kid—whatever their gender—fantasized about growing up to be—at least in terms of appearances. He was an idol—Dionysus incarnate. And the fact that he chose me to be his friend—that he actively sought my company—that made me feel like not such a loser after all.

I was working in this high-end rooftop lounge in the Meatpacking District when I met Bobby and Marco. They recruited me—made me feel special. And so, it started. We opened up a spot together. Bobby had the money. Marco had the charm. I had the experience. We were a team. Bobby was in charge of the business—in charge of making the place profitable. Marco was in charge of the party—in charge of making the place beautiful. He was the face of the place—the grand host. As for me, I was in charge of the booze—in charge of making magical drinks that tasted delicious and cost a fortune. I was a mercenary—slinging overpriced cocktails to wealthy wannabes.

The bar was a big success. Designed as an ancient opium den, we opened on Doyers Street—a crooked alleyway in the nerve-center of Chinatown. Huge crowds, loud music, pretty people, lavish marble, velvet booths, rare cuts of wood, antique medicine bottles, and alcohol—lots and lots of alcohol. And we made money. Really, really, good money. But I wanted more.

Bobby had a trust fund to supplement his lavish lifestyle. But Marco lived a high roller life too. And his wealth was a mystery to me. I couldn't figure out how he was able to live so extravagantly. At first, I thought maybe he was a trust fund kid too. Or had some secret sugar daddies somewhere. But as time went on, I sensed it was something else.

I'm a fool for not knowing he was dealing from the start. Because when I think about it now, it was so obvious. But I was naïve. So yeah, Marco was using the bar as his distribution center. A hip and crowded drug-hub in the lawless safety of Chinatown. It was brilliant. And Bobby and I had no idea. Marco was that smooth. But I finally found out one drunken night when Marco slipped up, and I caught him making a sizable deal in the back. The next morning—once we were both sober enough—I confronted him and asked him to cut me in.

That was that. I became Marco's side-kick. He handled the higher-ups and the cash flow. My job was to feel out new clients through the normal conversing that comes with being behind the bar. Like I said—as a bartender, you're a mercenary—a best friend and therapist working for tips. It's the perfect place to meet willing buyers. And Marco and I were more than happy to supply them.

Soon after, Marco and I started upping our game and pushing out more volume—recruiting underlings to work for us as small-time dealers. We created a network. Started to move even more volume.

Mostly we dealt in Coke, Oxy, Ecstasy, and Xanax. Our increased volume brought us the type of cash that allowed me to afford the lifestyle I'd always wanted. Bobby was happy because the bar was packed. Marco was happy because I was helping him make even more. And I was finally living that famous type of life. What could be better? What could go wrong? Well, of course, you know, when anyone in a story starts acting so cocky that they ask themselves these questions in all seriousness and without irony—then doom is certainly on the horizon.

∞

three

This is where Big Bad Boris comes back into play. Remember him? The drunk Russian guy who knocked me out? I wake up in his car, and I'm sitting in the front seat. This strikes me as odd, because I assumed kidnapping victims are always thrown in the trunk or restrained in the back seat. Then it dawns on me: I'm this guy's captive—I'm in trouble. Marco comes to mind—I bet this is about him. Something must've gone wrong. But I don't say anything. Just look around to get my bearings. My brain is still fuzzy. I notice that my seat belt is on too. This guy is strange. He knocks me out, but then is concerned enough about my safety to buckle me in?

We're driving over the Brooklyn Bridge, so I couldn't've been out long. Boris has an open bottle of vodka between his legs, and a gun resting on his lap. I wonder if he knows how much he reinforces his own stereotype? Regardless, I should be more concerned about who he works for and where he's taking me. But at this point, all I'm worried about is making it over the bridge alive. Boris is swerving and taking swigs, and it was only minutes ago he was chugging those loaded drinks at the bar—never mind what he drank before that.

I consider trying to escape. Punching Boris, stealing the gun, smashing the bottle of vodka over his head, grabbing the wheel, and crashing into the guard rail. Or opening the door and jumping out in a high-speed roll—action-hero style. Or just running out at the next stoplight. But I don't. I'd like to blame it on the punch to the face— some post-knockout impairment. Dazed and confused. But really, I'm just afraid—it's as simple as that. I'm afraid that whatever I try, I'll fail miserably, and he'll kill me. So I just sit there—silent and still.

The speakers are blaring Mariah Carey's "Always Be My Baby." Boris is singing along in a heavily accented falsetto using the vodka bottle as faux microphone, while at the same time intermittently honking and cursing in Russian. This would be hilarious, if it weren't for the fact that I'm his hostage. But the scene relaxes me enough to muster the courage to say, "You shouldn't be driving, you're too drunk."

"Victor!" Boris shouts out over the music, as he leans into me. The car veers. I slap my hands on the dash and brace for impact. Boris slams the brakes. We barely miss hitting the car in front of us. Horns wail. I sigh relief. But then my body tenses again. "How do you know my name?" I ask.

Boris smiles. "Good question, boychik. But I cannot tell you these things."

"Why?"

"How do you say in English, 'it is above my pay grade.'"

"Well, where are you taking me?"

"Another good question."

"Let me drive," I say. "You're drunk."

"Oh Victor, my friend, I cannot let you do that."

"This is about Marco, isn't it? This has something to do with Marco?"

"Sorry, above my paygrade, boychik."

"Well, I hope you die a miserable death," I blurt out.

"Now there it is. Your ferocity!" Boris laughs and shoves the vodka at me. "Here, drink. It will make you feel good." I take a swig and the burn does feel good. I take another sip. "I knew I liked you," he says, "I knew you had that American Ferocity. I think we could be friends. You know, under different circumstances."

"Yeah, best friends," I mutter.

"Don't be so upset, boychik."

"Well, I am upset!"

Boris laughs at my outburst.

"What's your name anyways?" I demand.

"I can't tell you. Above my…"

"Pay grade. Yeah, I get it. Well, I'm calling you, Boris. What do you think of that?"

"I like it! Yes, yes. Call me Boris. My Grandfather…his name was Boris."

The fact that Boris is amused by my attempted mockery only upsets me even more. But instead of channeling my anger into the dramatic action-movie style escape I imagined, I settle on making a snarky comment about his car instead. "Is this a compact?" I ask. "Jeez, Boris, I would've thought a tough guy like you would drive a big black Cadillac. Or at least a Lincoln."

Boris scowls, turns down his Mariah Carey, and looks at me. For a second, I think I've finally gotten under his skin. I hunch my shoulders and close my eyes, expecting him to thrash me with his gun. "Are you kidding, boychik!" he exclaims. "Do you know how bad the gas mileage is on a Cadillac? And how much the insurance costs? And how bad for the environment?"

"I didn't take you for an environmentalist, Boris."

But he ignores me, turns the music back up, and switches the track to "Fantasy."

We continue driving into Brooklyn.

Just my luck. I've been kidnapped by a drunk, diva-loving, eco-conscious, Russian thug.

∞

four

We pull into the driveway of a big Victorian house. I'd heard a neighborhood like this existed in Brooklyn, but I didn't realize the houses were this huge. It's got all the classic Victorian looks: three floors, a wraparound porch, and tons of windows. Also, one of those round spire rooms at the top. It's humungous.

Boris pulls around back, then leads me down to the basement door at gun point. So much for all the friendship and kumbaya. As we enter, my stomach churns and I swallow hard to keep from puking. Here we go, time for a beat down—for the leaky pipes, for the rusty chair, for the ropes and the saws and the torture devices. Time for Boris to work me over—give me the old one-two. Cut off a finger, or pull off a fingernail, or both. Maybe cut me up and make a skin suit out of me— Silence of the Lambs style—staple my face to his and prance around Central Park. All these possibilities are racing through my mind as he opens the door and leads me down some steps, then draws a curtain to reveal a warm, brightly lit library.

"Mr. Carroll, greetings and salutations to you!" says the man standing behind the curtain. He's an older guy, short and thin with glasses, and a big bushy gray beard. He looks like a history professor. "We've just been discussing you," he says. And then, over his shoulder, I see him: Marco! I knew this was about him. He's sitting in an over-sized leather chair looking awful—sweating and squirming like a kid caught cheating on his math test. I shoot him a 'what's going on?' look, but he just shrugs.

"Why all the mystery?" I say to Boris, "I specifically asked you if this was about Marco. You could have just told me this was about

14

him. Especially, if you were taking me to him. I mean, would that have been so hard?"

"Above my pay grade, boychik."

I've had enough of Boris and his banter. So I spit at him. Big mistake—he grabs me by the arm, twists it, drags me to the chair beside Marco, shoves me into it, and then bonks me on top of the head with the butt of his gun. My scalp erupts in burning pain and my vision blurs.

"Now, now, be magnanimous to our new friend. There's no need to be such an unwavering ruffian," the older guy says to Boris. 'Magnanimous' and 'unwavering ruffian,' who is this guy? And then, as if on cue, he chimes in and says, "Mr. Carroll, allow me to introduce myself. My name is Noah. Noah Horowitz. But most people just call me 'No,' because if you want something from me, chances are, the answer is going to be 'no.'"

I squint, then raise my eyebrows at Marco, as if to say, 'is this guy serious?' But he shakes his head at me, as if to say, 'don't mess with this guy.' But I can't help myself. I blurt out, "Wait, wait, wait! People call you 'No' because you say 'no' a lot? Is that your catchphrase or something?"

"I infer from your retort that you find my moniker unsatisfactory," he says.

"I mean, to be honest, it's just plain awful," I say. And I'm about to elaborate on why the name is audibly groan worthy, when Marco kicks me hard in the shin. It hurts like hell, but I take the hint, and shut my mouth. Noah strolls over to me and then bends down and studies me like some kind of research specimen. It'd be intimidating, if it weren't for the fact that he looks like a frail grandpa who enjoys building birdhouses and playing chess in the park. He leans back, removes his glass, gives them a spit polish, and smiles at me. "How about a drink ole sport?" Noah asks.

"Sounds swell, ole sport," I say. Why am I in a roaring twenties novel all of a sudden? But it only gets weirder. Noah goes over to his fancy bookshelf filled with leather bound classics and partially pulls one out. This triggers a secret door revealing a bar adorned with crystal decanters. He pours me a stiff shot of something amber and hands it to me. Marco is already holding a glass, but doesn't seem to be drinking.

"Let's have a toast," Noah says, "to our new arrangement."

We clink glasses and everyone takes a sip.

"What arrangement?" I ask, taking the bait.

"Indeed. I am very glad you have obliged me with this inquiry. Because now, we have arrived at the heart of the matter. Let us engage in a gentlemen's query of understanding. As you may, or may not, already be aware, I control the economy in which you and Marco engage. That is to say, you work for me. Furthermore, in addition to the inventory of goods which I supply to the marketplace, I also oversee the vast majority of wagers made in this city. And that is where the trouble arises. Your trouble, I'm afraid. You see, your friend Marco here has amassed a substantial debt."

Noah continues with his pompous explanation, but it's all clear to me now. Marco has a gambling problem. A huge one. That's his vice. It makes sense. Marco can have anyone and anything he desires. Life is a certainty for him. So he gets off on the one thing that's most uncertain—chance. And now, Marco is on the hook with Noah for a half a million dollars plus interest. And according to Noah, so am I. That's why I'm here. It's my job to make sure that Marco pays back his money. If he doesn't, Marco is screwed, and by extension, I'm screwed too.

The next question is: how're we supposed to get the money to pay back Marco's debt? Simple—at least in Noah's mind. Continue to deal for him, but for free—without a cut—until the debt is paid off. Plus, add an additional twenty percent for Noah's patience. Oh, and also, hit a weekly marker equal to triple our current volume. Let me say that again for dramatic effect: Noah expects us to triple our current volume! We are his drug dealing slaves. Although, he assures us this is a generous offer, because he doesn't usually make such "benevolent bargains" or "munificent deals." Finally, Noah concludes his villainous sermon by ordering Marco to lift up his shirt, which reveals fresh bandages around his flank. "A perfectly excised kidney!" Noah proclaims.

"What!" I exclaim.

"You see, Victor, there is no point in gratuitous violence. I do not believe in it. It is too savage. Too messy. And bad for business as well. Therefore, if you two fine gentlemen do not deliver on my directives, then I will collect my debts by harvesting your organs and selling them on the black market, and then using the rest of your remains as feed for my purebred canines."

I stare back at him. I look at Marco. I turn to Boris. Then back to Noah. I can't speak.

"I take it that you are astounded by my pronouncements."

"Well, I mean, I'm pretty sure you just said that if we don't pay you back, you're going to kill us, cut us up, sell our body parts, and feed the rest to your dogs. So, ah, yeah, I'd say I'm pretty astounded."

"Victor, it's going to be alright. I swear," Marco says.

"Indeed. The protagonist of our little melodrama has spoken," Noah says turning to Marco. Looking back to me, he says, "Marco here has already generously obliged to allocate one of his kidneys as collateral for our new arrangement. Depending on the current market rates, I will likely receive fifty thousand for that kidney in China. Alas, that money cannot, will not, count towards your debt."

"He really took out one of your kidneys? He's serious?" I ask Marco.

"It's cool. I still have the other one. You can survive with just one," Marco says as if this is reassurance that everything is going to be alright. As if this is some kind of silver lining, like, 'I caught my hand in a table saw and lost four fingers, but I still have my thumb'—that sort of idiotic optimism.

"Sure, you still have one kidney left," I say, "but that doesn't negate the fact that he surgically removed your other one!" At this point, it sinks in: we are in trouble. A memory pops into my head. Of falling off the dock into the lake as a kid. Before I knew how to swim. That same drowning panic courses through me now. Back then, my father was there to fish me out. But this time, there is no saving hand of grace. I wonder how many people will mourn my death. A minuscule number. The realization is brutal. I shoot down the rest of my drink, and ask Noah for another. He happily obliges.

∞

five

Big Bad Boris is kind enough to drive us back across the bridge, although he lectures us about climate change and complains about the cost of gas the whole way. At least, though, the blaring Mariah Carey helps drown out his rants about starving Polar Bears and the impending apocalypse.

When Boris drops us off at Marco's place on the Lower East Side, he gives us a sinister reminder about our debt, about what will happen if we don't pay up. And then a warning that if we try to run, we will have our assets frozen, our identities seized, and be hunted down and killed.

"Thanks for that reminder," I say.

"Well don't forget," he says. "And don't lose that American Ferocity, boychik."

"Yeah, yeah, I'll try to hold onto it along with my life."

"I'll be watching you," he says.

Marco's apartment is cool and sleek. A custom-built penthouse on top of an old tenement building on Essex Street. One of those super sexy all glass and steel joints with three-hundred-sixty-degree views of Manhattan. I told you, Marco has style.

When we get inside, we do the only reasonable thing that can be done—should be done—in this situation: we go right to Marco's private bar and proceed to get drunk. Marco gets wasted fast—both because he's a light weight, and because he's just had a kidney removed. In fact, a half a bottle of Mezcal into our bender, we have to take a timeout to change his bandages. They're soaked through with blood.

"You really shouldn't be drinking," I say.

"We're dead anyways."

We drink more Mezcal. Smoke a bunch. Snort some coke. And make lots of stupid jokes—busting each other back-and-forth. All of this with the intention of ignoring our dire circumstances. For the time being, it works. We're having fun, and feeling good and numb. Nothing like vice to block out reality.

Once we drain the bottle, Marco has built up enough courage to attempt an explanation and apology. "I'm sorry, I'm sorry," he slurs. "I've got a problem. A gambling problem. I like to bet. To bet on everything. Horses. Football. Baseball. I love to bet on baseball. It's a secret. A bad secret. And I'm sorry. For everything. I'm sorry. And usually, I'm so good. So good at winning. I win. I always win. But not lately. Lately, I've been losing. Losing big time. Losing so much. And I'm sorry. I'm really, really sorry."

"It's all good," I say, and give him a hug.

"I love you, man. I love you. Really man, I love you. I love you, Victor."

"I love you too, buddy. And I mean it, it's all good. Don't get me wrong. Tomorrow I'm going to be angry. Really angry. And afraid. Piss my pants afraid. But for tonight, for right now, it's all too much. You know what I mean? Better to drink it away."

"I'm sorry, man," Marco says again and begins to cry.

"Ah, come here, buddy, come here." I bring Marco in for another hug. A deeper one this time. He grips my shoulders. I feel his weight releasing into my arms. Feel the warmth of his tears trickling down my neck. My heart aches for him. And yet, it feels good to embrace him. To support him. To be trusted with his vulnerability. To be needed. To be loved. I pull away, and look in his eyes. "I asked for this," I say, "I asked you to cut me in. And you did. You don't owe me anything. We're friends, we're brothers. I mean, like I said, I'm still going to be royally pissed at you tomorrow. But we're all good. I mean it. Come on, let's get some fresh air."

We walk out onto Marco's roof. It's unseasonably warm for December. The sky is clear, the moon is full. A big fat chocolate chip pancake moon. We start howling at it like a pair of wild dogs. Howl and howl until our throats hurt—until one of the neighbors downstairs sticks his head out the window and screams at us. Marco and I collapse on the ledge and laugh like a couple of middle school trouble makers. We hang our heads over the edge and pass a joint back-and-forth. Down below, a guy and a girl are fighting outside the bar at street level.

"Baby, baby, baby," the guy is yelling.

"I jus' wanna drink," the girl is screaming.

"Baby, baby, Tina. Ya' drunk, baby."

"I just wanna drink. I just wanna cocktail."

"But baby, baby. Ya' drunk."

"You ah too."

"Hold on. Baby, baby. Hold on."

"Shut up, Sean! Just shut up."

"Baby, baby! Just let me speak my language."

"I saw you! I saw you talkin' to her."

"Baby, come on."

"I saw you. I saw you, Sean."

"But Tina, baby!"

"I saw you buy her a drink."

The couple continue like this. Marco and I watch enthralled as if this were a play staged just for us. That is, until the girl slaps the guy, and he shoves her into the brick wall behind them. She hits her head and falls to the ground. She seems okay, but struggles to get up. The guy tries to apologize—repeats a lot of "Baby, I love you" and "I'm sorry, I didn't mean it." But she doesn't buy it, and turns and runs back into the bar. The guy stays outside and lights a cigarette.

Marco and I consider going down there. But when we stand up, we get the spins, and realize we're far too drunk. Instead, we stagger into the kitchen and grab a giant mixing bowl. Then start grabbing random stuff from the fridge and cabinets and pouring it into the bowl. Milk, popcorn, tortilla chips, flour, coffee, ketchup, mustard, pickles, yogurt, and a few cans of beer. I'm surprised Marco has so much food in his apartment. Must be for when he brings his dates home. Because he certainly doesn't eat it. To keep up his physique, he follows what he calls the 'Rock Star Diet'—whole milk and cocaine. That's really all he eats, plus some salads here and there. Anyways, we mix all that stuff together in the bowl. It looks and smells foul. We carry the concoction back outside, splashing it everywhere in our stupor. At the ledge, we look down and are relieved to see the guy is still there finishing up his cigarette. He is talking to some new girl who is also outside smoking. We hold the bowl out over the edge and fling the mixture down below. It's a direct hit! The guy freezes in shock. We crack up laughing, then scramble off the ledge before he can look up and spot us. His yelling echoes through the street.

We lay on the roof and look up at the bleached city sky. Our shoulders touching. We pass a fresh bottle back-and-forth. Marco continues to take large swigs. I take small sips to oblige him. Anything larger, and I'll vomit. Marco leans his head into mine. "We're dead you know," he says, "there's no way we can move the kind of volume Noah wants us to move. Not in the time he wants us to move it. Not without taking risks and getting caught. But if we don't try, we're also dead. We're screwed—any way you look at it. I'm sorry I got you into this…"

"There's got to be some way we can figure this out. We've got to try."

"Yeah, there's no way."

"Then let's just run."

"No way. He'll track us down."

"He can really do that?"

"I know he doesn't seem like much, the way he looks and talks and all, but nothing Noah says is a joke. He's not to be messed with. He took out my kidney. So yes, he can find us no matter where we run."

"True. Very true. But we got to try. We got no other options. And if anyone can pull it off, we can," I say. But I don't believe a word coming out of my mouth. It just feels like the right thing to say. Someone has to be the optimist, right? Or else it would go something like this, Marco: "We're dead." Me: "Yup, we're dead." End of story.

"Hey! Let's go to a Yankees game in the spring," Marco blurts out.

I laugh. "Where did that come from?"

"Seriously, let's go to a Yankees game."

"I hate the Yankees. I'm from Boston, remember?"

"But I've never been. I bet on them all the time. But I've never actually been to a game. Let's you, me, and Bobby get box seats or a suite or something. Dress up in three-piece suits like they used to back in the day. Buy peanuts and Cracker Jacks. Drink beer and eat hotdogs. The whole package."

"With what money? The money we owe Noah?"

"Yeah, I see your point."

We both get quiet. Just sit there. Letting it hit us. Noah. The debt. The impossibility of the task. Boris. Our likely demise. The moon. The wind. The city lights. The illusion of baseball in the spring. The green grass. The crack of the bat. The roar of the crowd. A dream made more vivid knowing that day will never come. But it sure is nice to pretend. To forget about the world for a little while on this rooftop.

Marco jumps up and stumbles into the apartment. He comes back holding a bottle of something brown and ranting about, "no time like the present." He presents me with an unopened bottle of rare bourbon. "Let's drink it. All of it. Right now," he says.

"That stuff costs a fortune. And we're drunk," I say.

"I've been saving it for a special occasion. This is a special occasion."

"You're crazy. Opening it now would be a waste." But Marco doesn't listen. And before I can finish my objection, he has the cap off, and is slugging from the bottle. He insists that I share it. I take a sip and puke rises in my throat. "I'm sorry, buddy. I can't. Another sip and everything is coming up."

"Suit yourself," Marco says and walks away to the patio table to cut some lines of coke. I lay back down against the roof. I'm in that drugged stupor where you feel too drunk to talk, but too high to fall asleep. Marco snorts two lines and takes another shot. Then without any explanation, he strips buck naked and starts flapping his arms, making bird calls, and dancing around the rooftop. The bloody bandages wrapped around his stomach ripple in the wind. None of this seems odd in my current state. In fact, I try to applaud him, yelling, "Bravo! Bravo!" But I slur my words and choke on my laughter.

Then, I must black out for a minute. Because the next thing I know, Marco's standing on the roof ledge. He's taking swigs of bourbon while urinating into the wind. When he finishes, he stretches his arms out wide and stands up on his toes—arching his back as if he's readying himself to ascend into the heavens. Even though he's wasted, he moves with the grace of a ballerina. And then, sensing my attention, he turns back to me, smiles, and takes a dramatic bow, then looks up at me, as if awaiting my applause.

I start to clap. And then Marco is gone. Over the edge. Fallen.

The aftermath is fragmented. Me running to the ledge. Seeing Marco. Splattered. Yelling to him—even though I know it's no use. Panic. Tripping down the stairs. Seeing Marco. Twisted neck. No blood. Then a little pool. Phone calls. Yelling. Cursing. Flushing the drugs. Silence. Sirens. Lights. Tape. The yellow sheet over his body. Shock. A spider on the wall, while I give the police report. Grabbing the spider. Watching it crawl across my palm. Curling it in my fingers. Trapping it. Feeling its legs wiggle. Squeezing it—feeling a little pop and ooze. Opening my hand. Guts and legs. Smelling it—a sour stink. Licking it—foul vinegar. Smearing it across the brick. The cop looking at me like I'm insane. And all I do is smile at her. Play dumb about Marco's bandages. About why he was naked. About everything. I tell her that he slipped. That he got drunk and slipped. But I know the truth. Marco didn't slip. He jumped. He killed himself. Splattered himself across the pavement.

∞

six

Sleepless. Days. Nights. Daze.

I remember gathering for the funeral—lingering outside. Remember all the swaying steps, all the twittering thumbs, all the limp handshakes, all the awkward hugs. Remember the superficial small-chat with Marco's mother and father. Remember all faces I'd never seen before, all the faces I'd never see again. Remember Boris being there—watching me. Remember the congregation singing 'Amazing Grace.' The reverend talking about "the rapturous solemnity of death." Remember the phony eulogy by Marco's father. Remember everyone crying. Remember Bobby snotting tears all over my shoulder. Remember my girlfriend, Jinhee, sobbing into tissues, even though I know she hated Marco—thought he was a bad influence on me. Remember that even Big Bad Boris was crying—the irony of which was not lost on me. Remember everyone crying, except me. Call it shock. Call it anger. Call it fear. Call it what you will. But I wasn't crying. A sadness without tears. A jagged pit of sorrow in my chest.

Then, the mercy meal—filled with trite conversations and bad cold cut sandwiches.

And after all of it, Bobby and I go get drunk at the Turkey Neck Tavern back in Brooklyn. Bobby can drink anybody under the table. As I say this, I realize I haven't told you much about Bobby—besides him being the trust fund money man in our bar trio. So let me tell you a few things. Bobby is big and handsome—in a husky, middle linebacker sort of way. He has a mustache, and dresses like he's living in the seventies. Wears these finely tailored suits with his shirt open at the collar so his thick plush of chest hair sticks out. And that mustache—it's ridiculous,

26

but he loves it—it's a creepy type of thick stache that would make parents worry about letting their children near him. But he's a good guy—a goofy, fun-loving, party animal. Except about money. He's serious about his money. When it comes to finances, Bobby doesn't mess around.

After a few rounds at the Turkey Neck, Bobby and I go to the restroom. While we're in there, we do one of Marco's favorite pranks in his honor: standing at the urinals with our pants at our ankles. We stand there for what seems like forever waiting for someone to come in and see us. I start to get cold. But Bobby convinces me to wait. It's a bar, somebody's going to come in eventually. Finally, a drunk old dude comes in. But our bare butt cheeks don't faze him. In fact, he just looks at us and says to me and Bobby respectively, "Yours is rounder, but a little flabby. And yours is firm, but a little flat." Jokes on us, I guess. Bobby and I run out of there laughing. It's the sort of weird exchange that would've made Marco go wild.

We keep drinking. Bobby starts retelling our favorite Marco story. About the week we took off at the end of last summer. About how we rented a cherry-red vintage Cadillac convertible—Bobby knew a guy out in Queens who could hook up that sort of thing. About how we concocted a Gonzo-style road trip to Vegas. Racing across the country with a car full of booze, cash, and drugs—then gambling away our stash surrounded by gaudy glitz and glamor. But the story really begins on our way out of Vegas. Marco has us pull off at some random suburban exit. Next thing we know, we're driving through random cookie cutter neighborhoods and pulling into the driveway of a ginger bread brown house. Then Marco drops a bomb, explains that this is his house—his childhood house, his parents' house. Bobby and I are floored. We know next to nothing about Marco's past. He is all mystery and secrets—prefers it that way. Some nondescript pre-fab neighborhood in the Vegas desert is just about the last place I'd envisioned him growing up. But here we are.

And then he drops another bomb on us: his parents are religious—like speak in tongues, fire and brimstone kind of religious—and he hasn't seen or spoken with them since the day they kicked him out of the house after they found him fooling around with one of his classmates from the all-boys holy school. Bobby and I barely have time to register this information before Marco is out of the car and marching up the driveway. He's decided that today is the day for reconciliation.

When Marco knocks on the door, Bobby and I expect the worst. I'm hoping no one is home or that whoever answers just slams the door on us—that we won't be here long. It seems like we stand there forever. It's hotter than hell outside—it's Vegas in August after all. But then the door opens. Marco's mother. She hugs him joyously. Then she hugs me and Bobby too. Marco's dad appears behind his mom. He's gruff and mumbles some flat greeting, then shakes Marco's hand aggressively and nods at me and Bobby. It's surreal.

We sit down in the living room, and Marco's mom serves us iced tea, and makes pleasant chit-chat about the weather. Marco's dad sits in his leather armchair beside us, making call after call to family members and friends to share the news that Marco is home. I get the sense these calls are part of some plan—that Marco's parents have been preparing for this moment.

A dozen or so relatives and neighbors and church members show up. "Oh, how happy" they are that Marco has come home. "The Prodigal Son," they say. "The Prodigal Son has returned." And then more iced tea is brought out and passed around. We all make merry chit-chat and act as if Marco never left.

Marco's dad calls the room to attention, and asks everyone to circle around us and "lay hands" upon us in prayer. A giant group hug is formed with the three of us at the center. I'm hoping this is some kind of grand gesture of forgiveness. But then Marco's father starts screaming out an exorcism, "God Almighty in the name of your son Jesus Christ, combat the homosexual demons that possess these boys. Release them from their vile sins and bring them back into your flock. Release them O' Lord from the demons that possess them. Release them O' Lord from the wretchedness of their sins."

Definitely not a grand gesture of forgiveness.

The three of us are too shocked to move. The insanity builds. All the aunts and uncles and cousins and friends and church folk start speaking in tongues—rolling their eyes back in their heads, shaking their hands in the air, screaming out gibberish. Over all of this, Marco's dad keeps shouting out his sermon, "Release them. Release them, O' Lord." Building and building in fury. "Release them. Release them. By the power of Christ, release them." Building and building into an ecstatic climax. "Release them. Release them. By the power of Christ release them. Get out. Get out. You demons. Get out. Get out. You homosexual spawns of Satan. Release them!"

Then suddenly, Marco's dad stops his rant. He runs from the room. Everyone else gets quiet too. A garbage truck can be heard rumbling down the street. "Oh. Oh. We forgot to put out the trash. We forgot to put out the trash," Marco's mom says. And through the living room window, Marco's dad can be seen running the garbage cans out to the curb. "Oh shucks, we forgot ours too," says a random neighbor and they run out too. Bobby and I lock eyes. We grab Marco and get out of there.

Marco is quiet all the way to Denver. We try to cheer him up, but he won't have it. He just stares at the road ahead. I can't tell whether he wants to scream or cry or both. His face is red—he's holding his breath. We wait for him to explode. But then the Rolling Stone's "Sympathy for the Devil" comes on the radio. And Marco bursts into laughter. We all sing together and laugh.

Bobby and I continue laughing while we recount this story at the Turkey Neck Tavern. Our laughter turns into tears and we give each other sloppy hugs and condolences. Bobby is so much bigger than me that I end up sobbing into his sweaty chest hair. I almost blurt out the truth—tell him about Noah and Boris and the drugs and the debt, and about how, even though I can't prove it, I know Marco jumped, that he didn't slip off the roof—that he took the quick way out and left me his mess. But I don't. It's my cross to bear. Plus, Bobby wouldn't be sympathetic. If he found out that Marco and I were dealing out of the bar, he'd go apoplectic. He might even try to turn me in to the cops—he would definitely disavow me forever.

Bobby ends up puking in the bathroom. I've never seen him sick from drinking. I suppose this is his way of mourning. I pat him on the back while he spews. We both get teary-eyed again. But part of me is turning sour—cursing Marco for the trouble he left me. Bobby and I stumble out of the bar and waddle down the middle of the street with our arms slung around each other. We start screaming at the top of our lungs, "Marco, Marco, Marco!" And then someone, somewhere screams back, "Polo." Oh, how we laugh.

∞

seven

Jinhee's feet patter around the room. I'm pretending to be asleep—buried beneath the sheets with a pillow wrapped around my head. I took a cab to Jinhee's place last night after my debauchery with Bobby at the Turkey Neck. She was pissed when I stumbled in wasted. To my credit, I did try to be quiet. But I tripped taking off my jeans, and hopped then flopped across her bed, slamming my knee into her back. So when I started caressing her, she wasn't having any of it. I don't blame her—I wasn't exactly a prince in the moment.

Out of a slit in the pillow, I watch her walk around the room and get ready for work. Jinhee is better than me in every way. She's too good for me. Bobby has this game he likes to play when couples come into the bar on slow nights. Likes to debate who is winning the relationship. By winning, he means the person in the pair who is dating above their level. If you score a partner who is hotter or smarter or richer or funnier, then you've won. So with Jinhee, I won. She's smart, savvy, and sexy too—long neck, dark eyes, silky black hair. She went to prestigious schools and works a high-profile job as the press secretary for the district attorney's office.

We met at a swanky Spanish tapas lounge in the Lower East Side. I was working there at the time. She was having a hard time meeting guys she liked—work was mostly bosses and married guys trying to sleep with her. And so because she wanted a way to meet new people, she added to her already eighty-plus-hour work week by becoming the Sunday night hostess at the tapas lounge.

At first, she ignored me. But I persisted. Sundays were always slow. So I would sneak her free cocktails and champagne to pass the time. And use the drinks as an opportunity to talk. We bonded over *Of Mice and Men*. I told her about how I'd played Lennie in a high school production—it was during my "I'm going to get famous by being an actor" phase. It was our mutual love of John Steinbeck and my rendition of Lennie's desire to pet rabbits that won her over.

Jinhee is from a strict family—from conservative parents who expect her to marry a buttoned-up lawyer, doctor, or corporate type. She chose me because I'm the opposite of that. I'm everything her parents hate: an aimless bartender. She also likes my endless supply of drugs and cocktails. She must know about my dealings with Marco—she is too smart not to know. She's never once asked about it. But at some point, she must have wondered where I got the money for the drugs, clothes, and expensive restaurants.

Back in bed, my head is pounding and I'm thirsty. But I don't want to get up. I don't want Jinhee to know I'm awake. I know coming over late and drunk was a stupid move—and I'm sorry for it. But I also don't want a lecture. So I stay silent and still.

Despite my efforts, Jinhee knows I'm awake.

"Victor, I need to talk to you," she says.

I don't answer, hoping this is just a test.

"I know you're awake."

But I still don't answer.

"Victor, I know you're awake!"

"Huh, what?" I say, pretending her voice woke me up.

"I didn't appreciate you coming in here wasted last night."

"Sorry." My throat hurts and my voice is hoarse.

"I know you're upset about Marco."

"I'm sorry."

"Regardless, I want you to look at those job posts I told you about." This is Jinhee's big kick lately. She wants me to get a 'real job.'

32

This is her way of trying to change me—of transforming me into a suitable mate, into someone she can take home to her parents.

"Yeah, not happening," I say.

"There is an advertising job that'd be perfect for you."

I know she's right. I know she cares about me, and she's just trying to help. But the underlying insinuation that being a bartender is not good enough infuriates me. So I rip the pillow off my head and make a show of saying, "I'd rather be eaten by a swarm of flesh eating maggots than work in advertising."

"It's called a wriggle of maggots."

"What?"

"A group of maggots is called a wriggle."

"Whatever, you know what I mean." I pull the pillow back over my head. I shouldn't even care about this conversation, given the fact that I'll probably be dead soon—my body parts shipped off to the highest bidder in China. Although in some ways, considering my current situation, a cubicle job and spreadsheets don't sound too bad.

"Do me a favor," Jinhee says, "and don't stay in bed all day. I know you're sad about Marco, but you can't just lay around and wallow." She comes to the bed, pulls back the pillow and kisses my forehead. "I'll see you tonight. Or tomorrow maybe. Work's crazy," she says.

"Yeah, sounds good," I say. And she leaves.

I try to sleep. But thoughts of Marco haunt me. I keep drifting off just to wake up from the same nightmare—Marco beating me to death with a baseball bat. I don't have to be Freud to know the dream represents my fear about Noah and Boris, and my anger at Marco for offing himself.

Time oozes by as I lay there hungover. I stay in bed until noon. Mostly, I think about how as a kid, I'd stay in bed like this all the time, daydreaming about my future—escaping my trashy life in the suburbs and moving to the city, dating beautiful women, directing bigtime movies, making lots of money—being famous. I was always happy in those dreams. I imagined myself as an ultra-man: brave and strong and true. But right now, I don't feel like any of those things. Right now, I am afraid and weak and uncertain.

When I finally do get up, I take a shower. I love showering at Jinhee's place. I like using all her fancy soaps and scrubs and lotions. When I get out, I make funny faces in the mirror—beating my chest like a monkey, sticking out my tongue, and waving at my reflection. I grab and pinch the fat on my gut. I hate my stocky frame, soft belly, round face, and boring brown hair. I'm all-in-all not bad looking— just sort of average. But I don't want to be average. I want to be extraordinary. I am grateful for what I have—but I want more. That's the human curse, I guess—the very nature of suffering. We always want more and more.

Speaking of wanting—I'm hungry. I scavenge through Jinhee's fridge and cabinets. She only has healthy stuff like yogurt and granola bars and multigrain cereal pellets that look like rat turds. I'm craving a creamy cup of coffee and a greasy breakfast sandwich, so I head out to this diner I like a few blocks away. When I get outside, Boris is there waiting for me. I shiver when I see him. He's leaning against the hood of his car—parked right in front of Jinhee's building. It's snowing outside—the first snow of the season. But that's not why I shiver. If he is here now, that means he's been following me, that means he knows about Jinhee, that means she's in danger now too.

"Victor, my friend, I've been waiting for you," Boris says.

"Aren't you freezing?" I ask trying to act casual.

"I'm Russian," he says with a laugh, "I never get cold."

"Yeah, right, of course," I say.

"I saw your lady friend. She's nice. Very, very, nice," he says, and flashes a creepy smile—a smile that makes me fear for Jinhee's safety, a smile that suggests the pleasure he takes in violence.

"I was just headed out to get something to eat," I say, desperate to change the subject.

"Good," he says, "I'm hungry. We will go together."

Boris orders a double portion of French toast and drowns it in syrup. In between bites, he talks on-and-on about Mariah Carey— apparently, she's a real obsession of his. He tells me all about seeing her in concert back in Moscow, and how he cried when she sang "Hero" for her encore. I sit there and listen and eat my bacon, egg, and cheese—glad to have him talk about anything besides hurting Jinhee or killing me. You'd think I wouldn't be hungry, but I savor every bite of the sandwich.

When Boris finishes, he picks up his plate and licks the syrup off of it. Then he reaches beside him in the booth and hands me a black gym bag. It's heavy as hell. I look inside and it's filled with uncut blocks of coke and quart sized bags of pills. "What am I supposed to do with this?" I say in whisper as I look around the diner to be sure no one can see inside the bag.

"A deal is deal," Boris responds, "Marco is dead, so now it's on you."

"But I told you guys, I just sort of helped out. Marco used to cut and divide it all." I try to keep my voice at a whisper, but it rises in panic. "This is like, how do you say, above my pay grade."

"Well, boychick, you've been promoted," he says with a big belly laugh, "I believe in you. Remember, you have the American Ferocity. You have it!"

"What does that even mean?" I yell. People turn and stare.

"It means you can do it. And if you don't, then that's very, very bad for you."

"But that's the thing, I can't do it."

"You must, boychick. You have two weeks to sell this first bag."

"Two weeks! Can't I get a little more time than that? You know, considering Marco jumped off a building! And then left me all alone without any idea what to do. I told you, Marco used to handle all the technical stuff. I just helped him out."

"Ah, Victor, you must not have this type of attitude. Use your ferocity."

"But that's what I'm telling you, I haven't got any ferocity."

"You must. Two weeks. No exceptions."

There's nothing left to say. I pick up the check. I pay with the cash that I stole from Boris the other night at the bar. It's satisfying to do this—a sort of secret slap in the face. Boris gives me a lift back to my apartment in Brooklyn. He blasts Mariah Carey ballads and drives with the heat off to save gas. It's so cold in the car that my teeth start to chatter. And the drive takes forever because of the snow.

Back at my apartment, I drop the duffel bag filled with drugs on the floor, strip off all my clothes, and fling myself across my mattress. I curl up in the sheets like I'm wearing a toga. I'm exhausted. Panicked. Afraid. I stare at the plaster peeling off my ceiling. Listen to the *hiss-clink-clank* of the radiator. And drift off to sleep. Little league. A sunny spring day. Marco and Bobby and I in starched white uniforms playing catch and fielding ground balls. Having fun. But then Noah and Boris show up with bats. And Marco and Bobby pick them up too. And they all turn on me. Beat me. Shatter my arm. Crack my skull. I shudder awake. The bed is wet with sweat. I've only been asleep an hour.

I try to come up with a plan. I need a plan—desperately. But I can't think. So I do what I always do in periods of desperation, I watch my film—the one I made a few years back in film school, the one that was going to make me famous, the one that flopped. I watch this film

36

when I'm at my worst because it's a form of mental cutting. It's a tactile confirmation of my self-loathing—a physical manifestation of failure.

The film is called *The Suicidal Goldfish*. It's about a psychologist who keeps a goldfish in her office. Every day she arrives to work and finds it floundering on her desk. She can't figure out why it keeps jumping out of its bowl. The psychologist comes to theorize that the fish has become depressed from listening to her patients, and so is trying to kill itself by leaping out of its bowl. So the psychologist attempts to treat the goldfish for depression. The twist is that in trying to help the fish, she is able to heal her own issues. That's the intention anyway. But everyone who saw it asked, "Why didn't she just put a lid on the bowl?" It was a good question. The film flopped just like the goldfish.

I get out a piece of paper and try to write out a plan. But after a few minutes of scribbling, "sell or run or die," over-and-over again, I give up. So I spend the rest of the day getting high and watching old black-and-white movies in bed. I love the hardboiled detectives, the beautiful women, the terse dialogue, the snappy one-liners, the cigarettes smoking in crystal ashtrays, the brandy, the bourbon, the rye—the tough guys who solve the crimes and get the girls. A world of brute strength and blunt sincerity. I lose myself in it.

∞

eight

Snow drifts are forming in the streets. I walk to work to try to clear my head, to try to come up with a plan. The bar shouldn't even be open—closed out of respect for Marco. But Bobby is a tyrant about making money—so it's off to work I go. Besides, the routine is good for me. Plus, Boris or one of Noah's other goons are most likely watching me—and not showing up for work is a sure-fire way of getting myself killed and carved up. I am carrying the bag of drugs with me—probably a dumb idea to just walk around with it—but leaving it unguarded at my apartment seems worse.

Rainbow pools form in the potholes of the oil slicked streets. As I walk toward the bridge, I splash in every puddle I come across, and as the snow falls, I try to catch flakes on my tongue. The cold helps clear my mind. Although I still have no idea what I'm going to do, and thanks to Boris, I've got Mariah Carey's "We Belong Together" stuck in my head. I ramble past the graffiti covered garages, past the new condo construction and old clapboard houses, past cafes and galleries and tattoo parlors, past all shapes and sizes of restaurants and bars. The streets smell like bread and tar and dirt and roses. It's Brooklyn old and new.

I stagger up and over the bridge. At the halfway point, I stop to catch my breath. I get the spins, and grab the rail to steady myself. Despite the cold, I'm hot—my chest and back damp with sweat. A hangover is a harrowing thing, and I'm still reeling from last night. I look down. Breathe—long, deep breaths. And then I notice—a crooked line spray painted across the concrete. Someone has written "Brooklyn" and "Not Brooklyn" on opposite sides. And I'm straddling the line.

I stand atop the bridge—suspended—gulls circling and swooping around the spires, flapping white against the falling snow. Looking north, the City grows from the banks of the East River and rises up into the Empire State—its top lost in fog. Wrapping my fingers through the fence in front of me, I lift onto my toes—up and down, up and down—tapping my heels after each repetition—up and down. This would be a beautiful suicide. Plunging into the murky waters. Maybe it's my best option. Take my cue from Marco and jump. A barge hauling trash lurches toward the bridge, then recedes in the darkness.

I shake the thought of hurling myself off the bridge and turn to the abandoned sugar factory back on the Brooklyn side. Its outer bricks are covered in soot, its golden emblem tarnished, its windows shuttered. Sweet decay. I imagine what it must've been like inside the factory—what it would've been like to work there: laboring at a streaming conveyor belt, packaging millions of cubes into rectangular boxes, punching my card—clocking in-and-out—a modern machine and man. Sure, it would be a rough job, but still, there's something satisfying about it. Exhaustive labor that makes you so tired your mind can't haunt you.

The rumbling of the J-train rattles me from my daydream.

A biker rides by and splashes me.

"Hey!" I yell—but he's long gone and doesn't care.

Gray sky, red tail lights, tenement towers. I walk down onto Delancey Street. The traffic is horrendous. I'm glad I walked. Peking ducks hang in the window of a Chinatown restaurant. Warm and delicious. I stare at them and use this moment to check if I'm being followed. I can't tell. I'm getting paranoid. An old guy walks by and spits yellow snot into the snow. I turn up Doyers Alley and into the secret entrance to the Golden Dragon. Back to work.

∞

nine

I stand behind the bar staring out over a sea of drunken masses. Everyone is dressed in retro neon ski-gear for an event promoting some new alps-themed vodka. Their bodies shaking to the rhythm of trashy techno-pop being played by a hipster DJ in a snowman suit. Strobes flash and liquor flows. I work my way through a mad, never-ending wave of orders. Making, mixing, and shaking. Pouring and serving. Over and over. All the while, trying to figure out a plan. The music swells. The energy surges. The crowd roars.

I take a couple shots and watch the partyers slip on the synthetic snow—flapping arms and wobbling legs like first time ice-skaters in Central Park. The stuff was originally supposed to be part of the alps-themed party. The promoters brought it in by the box load. But the partyers tracked in real snow, wetting the fake stuff, and making the place like an ice rink.

Sliding on the synthetic snow, I reach out to serve a girl and her date. But as I do, my feet slip out from under me. My arms fly up, the glasses shatter on the bar, and I slam my hand down on a glass shard. I scream and shake my hand. Blood splatters—splotches landing on the girl and guy I'm serving. They shriek and groan. I rush back to the storeroom, grab a bottle of the alps-themed event vodka, pour it in a pitcher, and stick my hand in it. The burn is exhilarating. A red cloud inks out. Beautiful. Primal. I pull my hand from the pitcher and drink from it. One gulp. Two gulps. Three. I curl my lips and growl. Pound my chest. Grunt and wail. I'm a wild animal. It's all adrenaline. All madness. A vortex of pain and rage. Vodka, blood, and hysteria.

By midnight everything is chaos. The bar is hot and moist. The decomposing snow mixes with alcohol and sweat and makes the whole place smell like a rank salt marsh. Most of the partyers have stripped off their neon ski-gear. Hats and gloves and scarves are soaking on the floor. Everything is in disarray—broken glasses, dirty plates, melted wax, and assorted trash. The bathrooms are even worse—abandoned clothes, cigarette butts, half-smoked joints, and overflowing toilets.

I make drink after drink after drink. Obsessing about what to do. How to escape. How to survive. How to live. I'm drunk and tired and wounded. Bobby is wasted beside me, bopping his head to the music and pouring shots into peoples' mouths straight from the bottle. "What's the matter, buddy?" he screams over the music. "Let loose!"

"I'm dead," I yell into his ear. But he doesn't understand what I really mean by this, so he just smiles and laughs and hands me a shot. I take it, and as it goes down, it all comes together. An idea rises through the inebriation. I've got a plan.

∞

ten

Bobby has a little sister named Aubrey. She does some event-planning work for us at the bar. In fact, she's the one who organized this alps-themed vodka party. Aubrey has always had a thing for me. But because she's Bobby's little sister, and because I'm dating Jinhee, I've never acted on it. Until now. You see, she's a key part of my plan.

It's one in the morning. Aubrey and I sneak out of the party and leave Bobby and the rest of the staff to deal. Bobby is going to be pissed, but that is also part of the plan. We head to Aubrey's place in the Village. Drink some champagne. She's disappointed when I tell her I don't have any coke. Truth is, of course, I have a whole duffel bag full of it, but I'm not about to tell her that. A bluesy vinyl plays on the stereo. Her apartment is hot and dry. Snow continues to fall outside. We empty the bottle, the record ends, and I get up to flip it. But Aubrey grabs my arm. "Don't," she says, then gently takes my cut hand into hers. "Can I see it?" she asks.

"Sure," I say and unwrap the bar cloth I'd wrapped around it.

"It looks bad."

"It was worse before. The bleeding's stopped."

"Do you believe in reading palms?" she asks.

"No."

"I do. I had my palm read by a gypsy in Rome once."

"Oh. Well, what does mine say?"

"Some good stuff, some bad. Long life, no money," she says.

"Long life, huh," I say, "that's funny."

"Why?"

"Oh, no reason."

"Do you believe in love?" she asks.

"Why? Are you in love with me?"

"Oh no…no," she laughs. "I was just asking."

"Ah, I see." And I laugh too.

"So? Do you? Believe in love?"

"Sure. Why not."

"I think love is a finite thing."

"Okay."

"I think it's limited to a specific place and time."

"Okay."

"That love is just the intense desire of a singular moment. What do you think?"

"About what? Love?"

"Yes."

"I don't know. I fell in love once. And it hurt a whole lot."

"So you agree!" She straightens up and smiles.

"With 'what' exactly?"

Aubrey reaches out and runs her hand through my hair. I lean into her and close my eyes. She rubs my head and talks about her plans for the future. I relax into her touch and the sweet smell of her skin. For a moment, there is no threat or danger—there is no Noah or Boris. Marco hasn't died. There is no need to escape. Just this tender touch. Then suddenly, Aubrey stops talking and squeezes my arm with both her hands. "I have an idea," she says. "Come to Dublin with me!"

I open my eyes and sit up.

"Seriously! Come to Dublin with me!"

"Why?"

"To study Joyce. And the poets."

"Why?"

"Because they're 'The Greats.' And it's beautiful to be close to greatness."

"Do you feel close to greatness right now?"

"No, why?"

"Never mind—it was just a joke."

"Want to come with me? Want to come to Dublin with me?"

"Why me?"

"Because you're here with me now."

"Oh."

"Come with me. We'll have so much fun."

"It's a nice thought."

"What do you mean?"

"That it's pretty to think so."

"Wait. So do you want to come to Dublin with me or not?"

"Sure."

"Really!?"

"Sure, why not. We can leave tomorrow," I say. And then I lean in and kiss her, and she laughs, so I kiss her again, and she kisses me back. Her hair smells like honey. My mind clusters and my chest pulses. I think immediately about Jinhee—guilt. This is part of the plan, but still—horrible guilt. But then lust takes over. We slap our bodies together—clothes half-on, legs falling off the couch, elbows sticking into the creases. My hand hurts and I struggle. She whispers nonsense into my ear. We look into each other's eyes. Her stare is vacant. She is looking passed me. I'm just a character in a story she'll tell later about her wild youth. But I don't blame her. I'm nothing special. And besides—I'm not present either. We thrash and gasp and reach a sad conclusion. She sighs—most likely out of resignation. We slide off each other. I caress her hair, and she lays her hand across my chest. I wait for her to fall asleep. Call out her name and tap her a little bit to be certain. And when

I'm sure she's sleeping, I snap a picture of us together and send it to Bobby. I feel dirty about it. But it's part of the plan. Then I slide out from under her arm, throw a blanket over her, and kiss her forehead. Then I slip on my clothes, grab the duffel bag, and sneak out.

∞

eleven

"Stand clear of the closing doors, please." I race down the steps, jam my arm between the doors, and squeeze onto the train. It's surprisingly crowded and hot—the smell of sweat and body odor. Just after four in the morning—people heading home from the bars. I survey the car, looking for Boris or anyone else who may be following me. I hug the duffel bag of drugs to keep it safe. A teenage kid comes down the train car selling candy bars. He speaks in a mechanical drone that shakes my nerves and makes me laugh. "Good evening, ladies and gentlemen. I am not raising money for my school. I am not raising money for a basketball team. I am not on drugs. I am not homeless. I am selling candy bars because I like money. Money is good. Please buy my candy bars. One dollar, one bar—or six for five."

"Good for you kid," I say and give him five bucks.

I call and call Jinhee, ring and ring her buzzer, until she finally wakes up. She opens her door wearing a black robe with white polka dots. I will always remember that: a black robe with white polka dots. She looks at me with the wild eyes of someone who has just been shocked awake. Looks at me with the rage of person who has woken up like this two nights in a row.

"Really, Victor! Again?"

"I know, I'm sorry. But it's important." I drop the duffel bag and take off my shoes immediately when I enter—it's one of her rules. Her apartment reeks of cleaning fluid—bleach and orange zest. The floor sparkles. And I stare at it, while she continues to lash out at me for showing up so late again. But I'm okay with it. Anger will help. It's part of the plan. I give her the candy bars that I bought from the kid on the train as a half-hearted peace offering and then take a seat on her couch. She huffs at me and goes to the sink, fills the kettle, and sets it to boil for tea. She always makes tea when she's mad.

My chest is pounding. I need to do this, but it's going to hurt. "So. So. So. L-L-Listen." I stutter, "I messed up. I got drunk at the bar. You know Aubrey? Bobby's sister Aubrey? Well, you know how she's always had a thing for me. Well, I went home with her. I slept with her. And I'm sorry. I messed up. It was a mistake. And I'm sorry."

Jinhee stands rigid—her arms crossed, her face stern. She says nothing. Just stares. I can't look at her—but looking away is worse. So I bob my head back and forth from the floor to her eyes. She stabs the air with her fingers and opens her mouth as if to speak. But then stops. She takes a long, slow, deep breath. "I'm not going to give you the satisfaction," she hisses. She turns and crosses to her bed—ripping closed the sheer curtain that partitions her bedroom. The kettle starts to boil. It screams. I linger on the couch. Should I leave? This part of my plan is done. Mission accomplished: she hates me. But I can't stand her hurt—can't stand her pain. I get up, turn off the stove, and go to her.

"Jinhee, I'm really sorry, but…"

"You're a narcissist. A complete-and-total narcissist. You know that, right?"

"Yeah. You're right."

"You're a fool," she yells.

"Yeah, I am…" I reach out and try to grab her hand.

She scoffs and slaps it away.

"I'm sorry. Please…"

"Get out."

"I wish you could understand."

"Go. Leave. Now!" she screams and then shoves me.

I turn and sort of float away. As I pass the kitchen, I grab the candy bars off the counter. Not sure why I'm stealing them back—it's an impulse. When I reach the door, I look back for a moment, wishing I could explain, but there's nothing to say. So I sling the duffel bag over my shoulder and leave. My last image of Jinhee is her standing there furious in her bathrobe. White polka dots on a black robe.

∞

twelve

Outside the snow has stopped. There is a rare stillness to the city. Late at night. Blanketed in white. The sky bleached by artificial light. Traffic hums and the wind whispers through the streets. I hear a grunt and turn. In the covered entryway of the adjacent apartment building a homeless man squats—his pants around his ankles—using the doorway as a toilet. I try to avert my eyes, but he looks right at me. The guy shrugs and pulls up his pants. I shrug too—then walk over and give him the candy bars.

"Thanks. But you have any money?" he says.

I pull out the wad of cash I stole from Boris and hand him a hundred-dollar bill.

"Holy Mother!" he says. "Thanks a lot, sir."

"Consider it a gift from a friend."

"Well, what's your name friend?"

"Boris. My name is Boris."

"Thanks, Boris. I'm Hal."

"Nice to meet you, Hal. Take care of yourself, okay?"

"Always."

We nod. Go our separate ways. I walk on.

∞

thirteen

Okay, you're probably asking yourself: What kind of plan is this? Well, first off, admittedly, not a very good one. And even talking to you about it right now is embarrassing. But I need to do something—fast. So this is what I came up with: RUN. My only option, no matter how stupid, is to run. There is no way I can ever sell this stuff in time. Maybe Marco could have gotten it done, but not me. I thought for a quick second about going to the police. But if Noah isn't lying, and I don't think he is, then he'll find a way to kill me regardless of the police. So I've got to run. But that also means Noah and Boris will likely interrogate Bobby and Jinhee to find out if they know anything about where I've gone. I'll put them in danger. But when I saw Aubrey at the bar, an idea popped into my head. The plan is simple. Really stupid, but simple all the same. If I can make Bobby and Jinhee hate me then Noah might sense this and be more likely to believe that they have no idea where I've gone. Because I'm certainly not telling them. And what better way to breed hatred than by messing with my buddy's younger sister and then telling my girlfriend all about it. And look, even telling you this right now, I realize the idea is both moronic and cruel, but I'm desperate and my life depends on it. I don't have days and weeks and a team of experts to come up with a master plan. And I can't just leave them in jeopardy. With Bobby, they'll hopefully only rough him up a little bit, if at all. And with Jinhee, hopefully her job at the district attorney's office will protect her. But there is no real way of knowing. By running, I'm putting them at risk. But if I don't run, I die. So I just have to hope this works.

With that said, I've still got to figure out two more things: where to go and how to get these drugs back to Noah. If I take the drugs with me, I'm most certainly a dead man. And I can't just leave them on his doorstep or in my apartment with a note—though I did actually think about both of these options. I need to be sure he gets them back. Or else he'll be sure to hunt me down and kill me. So that's where I'm at.

∞

fourteen

Destiny's Salon is hidden in an old textile building down an alleyway in Tribeca. The entrance is unmarked. I press the buzzer concealed under the rusted milk pail that hangs beside the door. A series of bolts are unlocked. The door slides open. Billy Lee is standing there. "Victor," he says with a grin, "bring it in here brother." He wraps his gargantuan arms around me and lifts me off the ground in a bear hug. Billy Lee is a monster of a man—tall, strong, and wide. He's got a huge head made bigger by a ten-gallon cowboy hat. Cinched to his waist is a large machete with an ivory handle. He looks absurd—but I'm not about to tell him that.

"What's up, brother?" I say casually, as if it's normal to show up here at this hour.

"It's late. What're you doing here?"

"I was just out. Walking around."

"You know you can't be here right?"

"Yeah. Yeah, it's just. I need to see Destiny. It's kind of an emergency."

"Well you look awful."

"Really?"

"Yeah and what'd you do to your hand?"

"Just a bar cut."

"Ouch, bro. That must hurt."

"You think I can I come in?"

"You really shouldn't."

"Please."

"Well…alright. But just for a minute." Inside are the remnants of a textile factory—open ducts, hissing pipes, concrete floors, brick walls—that have been given modern renovations—fancy lights, silk

52

rugs, and expensive art on the walls. In the center of the room stands a large bronze sculpture of a naked woman kneeling atop a stag with giant antlers. The woman is rearing the stag's antlers back and drawing a blade across its throat. A gush of blood forever frozen in bronze.

Billy Lee has a small office off the main room. Inside is a desk with security monitors, a red leather couch, and a horse saddle hanging on the wall. I take a seat on the couch, and Billy Lee grabs a cigar box from his desk, opens it, and takes out some weed and rolling papers. As he starts rolling a joint, he rolls up his sleeve. "Hey, check this out," he says. He has a new tattoo—a cluster of trees and the silhouette of a boy on horseback. His skin is still red with irritation. The trees look like they're on fire.

"Looks great," I say.

"Thanks, brother. You see these trees, they're Southern Live Oak—they're symbols of strength—called Live Oak because they keep their leaves even in winter. And this horse, it's an Appaloosa—they have spots on them like a leopard. This one's name was Dorothy. She was my first. That's me riding her. Going to add more trees and some tall grass later." He finishes rolling the joint and passes it to me. I light it, take a long drag, lay my head back against the couch, and exhale.

"I wish I had a horse like that. Wish I could ride it into the woods. Ride forever," I say and pass the joint back to Billy Lee. "So um, is Destiny busy? You think I could see her, just talk to her for a minute?"

"Brother, she's always busy. But I'll ask." He takes a drag and picks up the phone. "Hey Dez…Victor's here…yeah, Victor… yeah, that Victor, he wants to see you…yeah…I know…okay…sure thing." He hangs up. "She says to give her ten. We have a VIP coming. Which reminds me, when he gets here, make sure you stay in here—that he doesn't see you. Confidentiality and all that."

A few minutes later the buzzer rings, Billy Lee gets up, closes the door, and leaves me in the office. But I can still see what he's doing on the security monitors. He opens the main door and a man enters. The guy looks familiar—fat, orange skin, big puffy hair—but I can't place him. I watch as Billy Lee escorts the man to a freight elevator in the back of the main room. When the doors are closed, Billy Lee calls back to me, "Okay, brother. You can come out now."

I open the door. "I know that guy. That's that guy!" I say.

"Come on, brother. I told you not to look."

"The security monitors."

"Ah! I forgot. I gotta stop smoking so much pot. Please don't say nothing to Destiny about it. Anyways, you should be all good to head up." And at this, he gives me another bear hug and sends me on my way.

Destiny's Salon is a legitimate salon during the day—Destiny is a renowned stylist. But at night, the salon is a high-end brothel. Destiny is a famous Madame as well. Yup, she uses her salon as a cover for an elite prostitution ring. I didn't even know stuff like this existed. But in a city of a million secrets, Destiny's Salon is one of the best. I met her through Marco. And since then we've become good friends. Talk about keeping interesting company.

The elevator doors open to reveal shining wooden floors. Destiny is standing against a marble desk holding two glasses of champagne. The salon is empty. The lights dimmed. Motown humming through the speakers. Destiny glides over to me and kisses my cheek. She is tall and strong—wearing a sequin dress. "Victor, baby," she says and hands me a glass, "what on earth are you doing here so late?"

"Where are all the people?" I had never been here after hours. I'd come for haircuts, but never any late-night activities. Even if I wanted to be a client, I couldn't afford Dez's prices.

"Oh baby, the salon stays the salon. Everything else happens upstairs."

"Oh, yeah, I guess that makes sense. Well, so, um, here's the thing…"

"Heard Marco's dead. You still hurting baby?"

"Dez, I won't lie. I'm in a lot of trouble. And I need your help."

"Sit down, baby. Sit down. Let me give you a wash."

"That's real sweet and all, Dez. But I don't have time. I'm in some real trouble."

"Baby, you sit down in that chair. I'm washing your hair. I don't care what you say. Don't care what kind of trouble you are in. You look haggard. Your friend just died. And I'm going to take care of you. I'm washing that raggedy hair. And what the hell happened to your hand?"

"Dez! Really, I'm…"

"I'm not asking, I'm telling."

"Fine. Fine. But I need you to hear me out," I say, and lean back in one of the salon chairs. First, Destiny changes the bandage on my hand—cleans and dresses the wound. Then she runs hot water over my head. I close my eyes. My body relaxes. Sam Cooke croons through the speakers. Destiny hums to the music as she massages shampoo into my scalp.

"Aww, wow. This is amazing. Thanks, Dez. Really. But I need to ask you…"

"Shh," she says and puts her hand over my mouth, "just relax." She towels off my head—kneading her fingers into my temple—then pats both my cheeks and kisses the top of my head. We look at each other in the mirror before us. Studying each other. Holding each other's eyes. She is wise and beautiful. Poised. I wish I had her strength and resolve. What does she see in me? Sadness? Pity? I can't bring myself to ask.

"There. There. That's much better, baby," she says. "Much, much better. You look human again. You look like you again." I nod in agreement. Destiny crosses back to her desk and pours us both another glass of champagne. We toast. Sip. "Now. Tell me what you need," she whispers.

"I know, you know, well at least, I'm pretty positive that you know, Noah. Yeah, that Noah. The Noah. Marco told me he's a client of yours. And well, Noah is my trouble," I say, and then proceed to fill her in on the story.

"Oh yeah, baby. You're in big trouble," she responds.

"That's not exactly reassuring, Dez."

"I call it like I see it."

"Yeah, I guess you do. But that's why I need to run. I have no other option. And here's the thing. I'm hoping I can leave this stuff with you. That's my big ask. That you can, maybe um, get this stuff back to Noah for me somehow. Because maybe if I return it, he won't try as hard to hunt me down."

Destiny smacks me in the head hard with a brush.

"Ahh!" I scream.

"Have you lost your mind? Oh! Oh! You have really lost your mind!" She spins me around in the chair and points the brush into my face like a dagger. "Victor, baby, this situation is bad, B-A-D, bad. And let me get this straight, you want to go and drag me into it? You have, honestly really lost your mind!"

"Please! I'm desperate."

"Yeah, I can see that!" she says.

"Look," I plead, "I can leave the bag with Billy Lee on my way out. I'll put a note in it. I'll say I've run off to Canada or something. Then you can act like you have no idea what's going on or what the situation is. Then you can call Noah. Just give me a few hours head start.

Then he'll get his stuff back. And you can tip him off about the note. He'll think you're trying to help him. And on top of all that, maybe he might actually think I've gone to Canada. And that will buy me some more time. Triple Win."

"Baby, you're sweet and all, but you're out of your head right now."

"I know it's not the best plan. But it's all I got. I have to go."

"Plan!? Your plan is going to get you killed."

"Please! I'm begging you. Please!"

Destiny shakes her head at me. I stay silent—stare at her, trying to will her to say 'yes.' She steps away from me. Lights a cigarette and pours herself another glass of champagne. And then, after a long drag and a slow sip, she says, "Baby, I can't believe I'm saying this, but I'll do it. You're a fool, but I'll do it."

"What! Really? Oh, Dez. Oh, Dez! Thank you. Thank you, thank you!" I jump out of my seat and hug her. I pick her off the ground and spin her. She laughs and slaps me on the head again with her brush.

"Put me down, you fool!"

"Oh, Dez! What can I say? You are saving my life here. Really. Saving it!"

"Listen baby," she says laying both her hands on my shoulders, "you need to take care of yourself. Be careful. Don't be stupid. I'm not convinced this plan is going to work. Noah is going to try hard to find you. Hunt you down. So you need to act right. Be careful. You hear me?"

"Yeah, I hear you."

"No!" She says and slaps my face playfully.

"You hear me?"

"Yes, I hear you."

"That's right. Act right. Be right," she says and kisses my forehead.

∞

fifteen

The sun is starting to dawn. The dry bone-chilling cold that follows a storm permeates the air. Wind blows snow drifts in waves and swirls. I wander South past Wall Street. Pausing at Ground Zero. American flags. Ragged memorials. New construction. Stark. Look around to see if I'm being followed. There is no one. I pick up my pace. Relieved to no longer have the bag of drugs wrapped around my neck like an albatross. Now I just need to figure out one more thing: where to go—where to run.

At Battery Park, I sit on a bench along the waterfront. Pink light stretches across the sky. The Statue of Liberty is poised in the distance. In all my time in the City, I've never once seen it in person. But seeing the statue now, surrounded by morning clouds and white-capped waves, I understand its power—its magic. It gives me hope. The promise of possibility. That maybe I might actually escape this mess.

Out of the corner of my eye, I catch the shimmering glow of wild eyes. I turn. A coyote. A coyote in New York City. It can't be. But it is. It's a coyote. Covered in mange, and bone thin. A beautiful creature all the same. We lock eyes. My heart swells, my skin prickles. Am I hallucinating? Losing my mind? I see it. Right in front of me. It comes closer. Moves cautiously along the rails. Moves so close I could touch it. "Hi there," I whisper. I reach out my hand. Unafraid. The coyote reaches out its neck. Touches its nose to my finger. Loud shouts erupt. I turn. A pack of drunken idiots come stumbling toward me. When I turn back, the coyote has vanished.

"Hey! You scared it away," I yell.

One of the guys struts up to me and shoves me, "Excuse me?"

His friends cheer him on to fight.

"Nothing. Nothing. Sorry," I say. But it's too late to deescalate. The guy knees me in the stomach. I slump over on the bench and pretend to hit my head and pass out—go full possum—a move I learned when I was younger in order to escape playground bullies. The guys freak out, afraid they might have killed me, and run off. I sit up—alone again—and begin to cry. Hot, startling tears. Because of getting jumped by those jerks. Because of the coyote. Because I'm overwhelmed. And afraid. And desperate. Like the coyote. Scavenging to survive.

I make a decision. Something I don't want to do. But something I need to do. It's my only hope—he's my only hope. I grab my phone and make the call. He answers right away. We make idle chit-chat. It takes me a few minutes to say it. But finally, I blurt it out. "I need your help, badly," I say. He doesn't hesitate. "Come. Now. I'll pick you up at the station," he says. And with that, I hang up, and throw my phone over the rail. It splashes into the water. No way to be traced or reached. I blow the Statue of Liberty a kiss and wave goodbye. I'm going home.

∞

sixteen

I enter the bowels of the City—the Port Authority Bus Terminal. I buy three different tickets from three different windows—one to Montreal, one to D.C., and one to Maine by way of Boston. Pay all in cash. I'm still not certain how well, or how much, Noah can track me, but I'm not taking any chances. And I'm hoping that when Noah sees the note I left with Destiny, that he'll take me at my word, and believe I ran to Canada. Probably not, but worth a shot. No matter where I run, Boris will most likely be close behind—ready to carve me up to the tunes of Mariah Carey.

I have an hour to kill before the bus boards, so I get in line, and lean against the red-tile wall outside the departure gate. I keep my head down and try to look anonymous. The whole area smells like urine. There's a row of vending machines across from me, and I pass the time by trying to guess what people will buy based off their appearance. I'm amazed at how accurate I can be: Frat boy—Snickers Bar. Fat guy with a ponytail—Doritos. Skinny punk girl—pretzels.

A little boy buys a bag of chips and they get stuck in the machine. He starts kicking and punching at the glass. His parents are nowhere to be found. A man turns the corner and barely misses getting kicked in the nuts. Don't know if this guy is the kid's father or not, but he tries to help get the chips and begins rocking and shaking the machine. The back legs of the machine start to come off the ground. An image flashes of the machine falling and smashing the kid. So I jump out of line, go up to the machine and buy a bag of the same chips. Two bags fall. I grab them and give one to the kid and one to the other guy. The kid grabs his and darts away. The man mumbles, "Yeah, thanks," and then wanders away as well. A small crowd has gathered to watch this scene play out—so much for going unnoticed.

When the gate opens, I board the bus and head straight to the back. I sit on the aisle of an empty row, and spread my legs and arms out wide and shut my eyes—hoping to prevent anyone from sitting next to me. It's an obnoxious move, but I don't want a big sweaty guy cramming in next to me. But the bus is sold out. So eventually a skinny, druggy looking dude taps me and asks to "squeeze in." I avoid eye contact and get up without responding—trying to avoid any opportunities for small talk. Sit back down. Close my eyes. The bus beeps. Reverses. Accelerates. And I pass out into oblivion. More baseball dreams. Ground ball. Double-play. Homerun. Celebration. Marco smashing my teeth out. A broken bat impaling me.

I jolt awake and realize that I've had my head resting on the dude's shoulder next to me. My mind is cloudy and my mouth dry. "Ah. Uh. Sorry. Sorry. Excuse me. Sorry," I say.

"No worries, man." The guy has dark eyes, a gaunt face, and a patchy beard. He's wearing torn jeans and a leather jacket. He's got a brown paper bag open on his lap and an open shooter of Jack Daniels in his hand. "You were out cold there for a while, man," he says, "I nudged you. But you wouldn't budge."

"I'm sorry. So sorry. I'm embarrassed."

"No worries, man. I know the feeling. Seems like you needed it."

It's hot—stale. The bus lurches and stops, lurches and stops—stuck in traffic on the highway. There must be an accident. I wipe my face. My chin is wet. "Aw! Was I drooling?"

The guy touches his shoulder and laughs. "No worries, man. Just a little damp."

"Oh man. I'm sorry."

"Nah. Man. Nah. I didn't even notice. Trust me, it's all good."

"I am so, so sorry."

"Come on, man. Stop apologizing already. It's all good. I'm Neal by the way."

"Victor."

"Good to meet you, Victor."

"Where are we?" I ask.

"We just got on the Mass Pike."

"I must have been out for a while then?"

"Yeah. I'd say at least a couple hours."

"Felt like forever."

"Drink?" Neal asks and tilts the brown paper bag on his lap towards me. "I got myself a buffet." The bag is filled with a dozen or so different shooters. "Here. Take a few." And he rattles the bag at me.

"Sure. Why not." I reach in to grab a few.

"Wait. I like to make it a surprise," Neal says, pulling the bag away from me. "Close your eyes, reach in, and pick one. It's better that way. Not knowing."

And like he says, I close my eyes, reach my hand around in the bag, and pull one out.

"What'd you get?" Neal asks.

"Rum."

"Nice."

"Well, cheers," I say, uncapping the bottle and taking a sip.

"Nah, man. No sips," he says. "You have to shoot it. That's the game."

I look at him—uncertain if he's serious. But he nods his head and gestures at me to shoot it. So I do. The rum warms my belly. Feels good. This guy is a strange character. But I like him. And appreciate the free booze. And the distraction.

"Alright, my turn," Neal says. He makes a show of closing his eyes and reaching his hand into the bag. "Eeny, meeny, miny, moe, catch the tiger by the toe, if he hollers let him go, eeny, meeny, miny, moe—my mother says to pick the very best one, and that is Y-O-U!" He pulls his hand out of the bag and opens his eyes. "Damn!"

"What?"

"Tequila."

"What's wrong with that?"

"I hate tequila."

"Why'd you buy it then?" I laugh.

"All part of the game, my man," Neal says. Then opens the bottle and downs the tequila. When he's done, he offers me the bag again. I reach in and pick out a bourbon. Neal picks again too—a vodka this time. "So where are you headed?" he asks.

"Home," I say, "I'm getting off in Boston." And as soon as I say it, I regret it. I shouldn't be telling anyone where I'm going. But Neal seems nice—trustworthy. So I roll with it. "Where're you going?" I ask.

"Boston too—I'm from Dorchester," Neal says, "I go down to New York once a month. Doing this study. Get this. I get drugs for free. Ecstasy. Legally and everything. It's supposed to help with these messed up dreams I got. I was in Iraq and all."

"Yeah, I get messed up dreams too. Especially lately."

"Were you in the Marines?"

"Nah."

"Too bad. Else, I'd say you should do this study with me."

"Is it helping? The Ecstasy?"

"I mean, kind of. I mean, I'm not supposed to be drinking. But…"

"Yeah, I get it," I say.

Then suddenly, Neal stops talking. Gets this flat look in his eyes. He turns and looks at me—a deep stare that makes me avert my eyes. "I'm going to try sleep now," he says in monotone.

"Yeah, sure, of course," I say.

Neal turns and looks straight ahead. He doesn't close his eyes. Doesn't even seem to blink. Just stares. His sudden mood change gives me the creeps. Maybe he's got PTSD. Maybe I triggered something. Regardless, I'm glad to leave him alone. It's best for me to stop talking.

The bus pulls into South Station in Boston. Both Neal and I get up and walk down the aisle without speaking. But as I step off, I turn back to him. "Hey! It was nice to meet you. Good luck," I say.

"Yeah, likewise, man," he says and extends his hand. We shake hands. We walk through South Station side-by-side, but in silence—feet apart, worlds away. We exit the station, nod to each other, and I watch him walk away.

The air is cold and biting. The streets are crowded. People coming and going. Cars picking up and dropping off. A hive of energy. I look around, but I don't see him. I feel a tap on my shoulder. I turn. Standing in front of me is an image of myself—waiting for me—my twin brother.

I'm home.

Part Two

∞

one

Liam gives me a hug. And we walk to his minivan. Liam is who I called before chucking my phone into the water at Battery Park. The guy who I didn't want to call, but is the only one who can help me. My twin brother—Liam. We are identical—well, we used to be. Now, he looks much younger than me—clean shaven, clear skin, cropped hair, and no bloat—less drinks, drugs, and late nights. Also, Liam is a Catholic priest. I buried the lede on that one. He's dressed in all black and wears a white clerical collar. Talk about two people coming out of the womb identically, but living in the world as polar opposites.

"Thanks for picking me up," I say.

"What happened to your hand?"

"It's the Stigmata. Jesus called me to serve as well."

"Come on, Victor."

"It's just a bar cut."

"How'd it happen?"

"Well, I cut my hand at the bar."

"Yeah, but…nevermind."

A horn wails. A taxi driver curses at us for idling too long. Then wails on his horn again. Something snaps inside me. I walk up and slam my fist on his hood. He hits the horn harder.

"Yeah, yeah!" I yell.

The driver rolls down his window—swearing at me.

I slam my fist on the hood again—and curse back.

"Victor, stop it, please," Liam says.

The driver continues to honk and scream.

"Oh yeah! How about this?" I say then turn around and pull down my pants and moon him—rubbing my bare butt across his hood.

"Victor! Knock it off. Let's go!" Liam yells.

The cabbie screams—and starts to get out of his car.

I blow him a kiss and run for the van. Jump in and we speed away.

We ride in silence through traffic. Liam exhales loudly and shakes his head. He fidgets with the wooden crucifix around his neck. Rubbing it and murmuring—praying—reciting 'Hail Mary.'

"What are you praying about?" I ask.

"I'm praying for you."

"Please don't."

"You want to tell me what that was all about back there?" he asks.

"That guy was jerk."

"And so were you!"

I flip on the radio. The sports radio station hosts are blathering about the chances of the Patriots winning the Super Bowl. I turn to Liam. "Sorry," I say, "sorry about that. And thanks again for picking me up. I appreciate you being here. Really."

We merge onto Route 1.

∞

two

Liam and me. We have old wounds.

The first eleven years of our life were good. Our father was a great guy—a fireman. He loved us—and we cherished him. Everyone loved Pap. He was all love—a big, kind, grownup kid who loved to laugh. He had this big wild laugh. Like a roaring cackle. And when he started, he just couldn't stop. It was infectious. Ask anyone who knew him, and I bet you the first thing they mention is his laugh. If you needed some joy in your life, you just needed Pap to laugh.

But then one-day, Pap had a few too many beers at the bar and smashed his motorcycle into the side of an eighteen-wheeler. He died on impact—his body severed in-half. As a kid, I was obsessed with all the gory details of his death. Some bizarre coping mechanism. I loved telling people about it. Making them squirm with gory specifics about his intestines slithering across the road—his blood pooling on the asphalt like hot molten lava. I never actually saw his body at the scene. Just imagined it. Rendered it in vivid detail. Played it over-and-over in my mind. And then recounted it to anyone who would listen.

After Pap died, our mother lost it. She got real mean and real drunk. To be honest, Mom was already a lush—already strict and quick to anger. But with Pap gone, she got extreme. Barricaded herself in her room surrounded by a wall of cheap boxed wine. Rarely left her bed. Barely ate. Drank all day. Watched talk shows and soap operas. Pissed in buckets that she made me and Liam empty. Got angry and beat the crap out of us.

Mom never beat us while Pap was alive. She would yell at us. Scream at us sometimes. She would spank us and slap us. One time she even hit me with an open palm to my bare back so hard that her hand print stayed there for two days. But I thought it was funny, because I got to stay home from school on account of Pap thinking someone might see it, and report us. Nothing Mom did ever amounted to real violence in my mind—to abuse. But after Pap died, she made a sport out of beating us. Eyes wet with wine, mouth seething, skin red with rage, she would whip us bloody with wire coat hangers. I don't know why she liked those hangers so much, but they were always her weapon of choice. I got the scars to prove it.

Liam got it worse than me. He's more sensitive. That set Mom off. She called him her "Little Nancy Boy." I used to throw myself over him and try to take the brunt of it. But sometimes that made it worse. There was a period of time when we were twelve that we were getting whipped a couple times a week. One time she even beat our cat. He tripped her on her way to the bathroom. And so she kicked him into the wall. But Patches got the last laugh on that one. He bounced off the wall, landed on his feet, meowed, and took a giant dump on the carpet. He never did walk the same after that though.

Mom worked part-time as a real estate agent. But soon, she was too drunk to work at all. So we lived off her savings. And after that dried up, she pawned stuff for cash. But sometimes that meant no electricity or heat. Sometimes no food. Liam and I fended for ourselves alright though—our favorite meal was white bread and mayo sandwiches. 'Triple Whites' we called them. I've made more of those sandwiches in my life than any other thing. Anytime Liam was upset about something Mom said or did, I'd make him a 'Triple White' and it would cheer him up. The creamy tang of mayonnaise mixed with the sweet, spongy white bread. They were delicious.

The beatings continued off-and-on for about two years. Then one night, just after our 13th birthdays, mom gave us both a brutal whipping. The scars on our backs broke open. Blood soaked through our raggedy white t-shirts. And something snapped inside me. I couldn't take it anymore. I went into the garage and took a hammer from Pap's old toolbox. Then I marched into Mom's room and smashed her TV with it. Put it right through the glass. Told her I would kill her with it—bop her right over the head—if she ever touched us again. She cried in horror after that.

We ate a lot of 'Triple Whites' that night in celebration. Stuffing our faces and stomping around in hysterics—reenacting the smashing of Mom's TV. Laughing and listening to "Maxwell's Silver Hammer" on repeat. Replacing Maxwell with my name as we sang. Laughing so hard we choked. We didn't even feel the pain. *Abbey Road* was Pap's favorite album. And he loved that song. Now it was our favorite too. That's one of my happiest memories. And Mom never laid a hand on us again.

Liam and I had our falling out about fifteen years ago. I skipped town and set out to be famous as you know. It was my way of coping with the trauma. Liam found God and became a priest. That was his way. But that wasn't what caused our riff. It was the fact that after he got ordained, he decided to forgive Mom. Not only that, but to take care of her too. To pay for expensive treatment programs that never worked. Never worked because Mom didn't want them to work—because she wanted to drink. And then when karma struck, and Mom got diagnosed with early onset Alzheimer disease, Liam goes and pays for her to live in a fancy nursing home. I couldn't understand—I still can't understand—how he could ever forgive her. Why he would take care of her and pay for her treatment. It's unfathomable to me. Infuriating. So much so that we haven't spoken in nearly a decade. Until today.

three

We pull into the parking lot of Chow-Eats Chinese Restaurant. We used to come here as kids for birthdays and special occasions. We celebrated our eleventh birthdays here, in fact—about a month before Pap splattered himself across the highway.

"Figured we'd grab a bite to eat," Liam says as he backs into an empty spot.

"Can't we just go home? I'm exhausted."

"We need to celebrate you being home."

"I hate this place."

"You used to love this place."

"No, you used to love this place."

"Oh, come on, Victor! Give up the animosity."

"Look. I really shouldn't be seen in public."

"Fair enough." Liam gets out of the van and leaves me sitting there. I wait for a second, hoping my refusal to move will make him reconsider. But he walks into the restaurant without looking back. I am not just going to sit in here and wait for him to eat without me. So I pop off my seatbelt, open the door, and follow him inside.

Chow-Eats is an extravaganza—a monstropolous modeled after the Forbidden City. A floor-to-ceiling saltwater fish tank greets you in the lobby, followed by glossy black floors and rows of big red booths. Faux marble stairs lead up to the second floor, where a balcony with tiki tables looks down over a bar that encircles a giant golden flaming dragon statue. We always sit along the balcony. Pap liked to be able to look down and watch the crowd.

"I'm not hungry," I say as we look over the menus.

"Well, I'm paying, so get whatever."

"In that case, I'll order double."

"Go for it. Leftovers are always good."

The waiter arrives. Liam orders tea and Kung Pao Chicken. I get nothing.

A gong rings out. This signals the start of the famous Chow-Eats challenge: General Tso's War. The goal is to eat seven pounds of General Tso's chicken, a large plate of fried rice, and a fortune cookie in under thirty minutes. It costs fifty bucks. If someone finishes in time, they get their meal for free, their picture on the wall, and a t-shirt that reads: "I defeated General Tso's Army at Chow-Eats Restaurant." A guy in one of the booths on the lower level is doing the challenge. Liam and I watch him. Use this as an excuse to avoid talking. But after ten minutes, when it's clear that there's no way the guy will ever finish in time, Liam turns to me and says, "So you want to tell me what's going on?"

"Yeah. Yeah, I do," I say. Then I take a deep breath and tell him everything. About Marco and Bobby. About Boris and Noah. About Jinhee and Destiny. Even about Neal on the bus. About the bar and the drugs and the suicide and the ultimatum and all the trouble. About seeing the coyote and getting jumped. About being hopeless and afraid. About calling him. About needing him.

I finish. And after a few slow sips of tea Liam looks up and says, "First and foremost, whatever you need, I'll help in whatever way I can. But I've got to say, this is very serious stuff, Victor. And well, honestly, none of it really surprises me. I've been expecting something like this from you for a long time."

"What's that supposed to mean?"

"It means that your behavior has been trending in this direction for a long time."

"A long time…we haven't spoken in like ten years!"

"I'm just saying that none of this surprises me, that's all."

"Well, aren't you a self-righteous holy-rolling prick of a priest all of a sudden."

"Geesh. I'm sorry I said it. And I do want to help."

"Well, how is that helping? I might be a dead man soon. And you decide now is the time to do some kind of confessional character analysis with me? You know, as I was just sitting here telling you all this crap, I was thinking about how much I miss this. Talking to you. Thinking about when we were kids in our bunkbeds. Remember. How I'd lay on the bottom bunk and talk up to you for all hours of the night. You just laying up there laughing. I'd forgotten how much I used to love that. Talking to you. Guess I was wrong."

"I'm not trying to attack you. And I do really want to help. All I'm saying is that if you really want help, then you should consider your actions and behavior. Consider how you got into this mess in the first place."

"All I want to consider right now is how to get out of this mess! How I got here really doesn't matter if I'm dead in three days. And right now, I'm asking for your help. To help me figure out how to escape. And so far—all you've done is sip tea and tell me I'm a jerk."

"That's not…"

"Hey, man! Over here." I cut Liam off and holler at our waiter.

"All I'm trying to do…"

"Forget it," I say, and then turn to the waiter. "Hey man, let me get one of the General Tso's Challenges. One of those fifty-dollar joints. My brother over here is paying the tab, I'm going to go ahead and give it a whirl. And let me get a Manhattan as well, please. Thanks a lot."

"Why are you doing that?" Liam asks as soon as the waiter is out of earshot.

"When in Rome. Or in China. Or wherever, I guess."

"Seriously. Why?"

"Why not? I'll consider it a last meal."

The food comes out in a big bamboo bowl—all seven pounds of it.

"You have thirty minutes," the waiter reminds me.

"Yeah. I got it, thanks," I say. Liam shakes his head again and mutters prayers to himself. The waiter wheels up the giant gong and places a big red timer on the table. "Okay," he says, "1…2…ready…go!" The gong rings, and I start stuffing my face. A woman at the next table snaps a picture—I smile widely at her.

I start off at a steady pace. The food tastes good—turns out I am hungry after all. I eat with efficiency—forking single pieces of chicken into my mouth and chewing just enough to swallow—taking small sips of water after every few pieces. Seven minutes pass and a big chunk of the chicken is gone. Maybe I can actually do this. I'm even feeling confident enough that I stop for a few sips of cocktail too.

"You're going to make yourself sick," Liam says.

"I got this." But things start getting tough at the fifteen-minute mark. The hardest part to get down is the cloying sauce that sticks to the chicken. It makes my tongue numb. But I keep eating—piece after piece. With only five minutes remaining, I finish the chicken. But I still have to eat all the fried rice. And the fortune cookie too. I'm stuffed. Each swallow starts to hurt. But I'm determined. The rice is dry and makes me gag. I try adding some soy sauce to lubricate it. But that just weighs it down. So I start shoveling in spoonfuls and using water to choke it down.

With two minutes remaining, the tables around us turn and start cheering. I'm sweating and may vomit. "Go buddy! Go! You can do it," a neighboring table chants. But I can't, I'm too full. "Go buddy! Go! You can do it!" they yell. I can't. Each bite is poison. "Go! Go! Eat! Eat! Eat!" the cheers grow. Liam looks on—aghast. One minute remains. A quarter plate of rice and the fortune cookie are all that's left. I take another bite. Close my eyes. Swallow. Gag. The rice comes back up. But I catch it in my throat. Swallow hard—gulp. Force it down. It burns.

"Victor. Stop. This is disgusting. You're making me sick," Liam pleads.

"Go! Go! Eat! Eat! Eat!" the crowd continues. I shovel more rice into my mouth. Thirty seconds left. "Go! Go!" the crowd chants. "Stop! Stop!" Liam shouts. I shovel more. Ten seconds. Just a few more bites and the fortune cookie. I smash the cookie on the table and throw it in with the rice. Just a few more...

"Time!" the waiter yells as he rings the gong and the buzzer sounds. A handful of rice and the crumbles of the fortune cookie remain on my plate. I lost. The crowd groans and returns their attention to their own meals.

"Can we get the check please?" Liam sighs to the waiter.

I pick the fortune out of the bowl, flicking off the flecks of rice stuck to it. "You Must Try—Or Hate Yourself for Not Trying," it reads. Wise words, I suppose. The waiter returns with the check. Liam shoves it across the table. "To be clear," he says, "I'm not paying for this."

∞

four

The sky is gray—winter dusk. Black grime covers the snow heaves along the highway. Liam drives slowly in the middle lane. Cars zoom past us. Liam has always been this way—nervous, cautious. I'm so full and uncomfortable that I can't sit. So I'm sprawled out across the back row of his van. I'm fidgeting—can't settle. I'm ill. From the food. From the stress. Noah knows I'm gone by now. Boris is probably on my trail. Bobby must be wondering where I've gone too—fuming over the picture I sent of Aubrey. Jinhee hates me. And I might have just eaten my last meal.

Sports talk is blaring on the radio again. The latest debate is whether the Patriots will go undefeated. It's a perfect distraction. Liam doesn't even like sports or football, but I know he's listening for the distraction as well. It's comforting. Nostalgic. It's all Pap ever played on the radio when we were kids. In the car, in the house, in the garage working on his motorcycle. These know-it-all talking heads are audible memories of Pap—the sounds of home and family and love. And it's always good for a laugh. Like when "Mary from Medford" calls to complain about Tom Brady wearing gloves in the last game. "He looks like a debutante out there," she says in a heavy smoker's rasp, "it's not like there was a Nor'Eastah or something. He's gotta' be toughah then that."

A jingle for a local charity comes on during the commercial break. It's about donating old cars to fund a charity for kids. It's annoying but so catchy that I can't help but start singing along aloud. Liam joins in too. We sing louder and louder. Laughing. It breaks the tension. And when the commercial is over, Liam turns off the radio, and looks back at me in the rearview mirror.

"I'm worried about you," he says. And waits.

"Thanks. I appreciate that. Really, I do. But I'm fine," I say.

"You are clearly not fine."

"Well, I will be fine."

"Will you?"

"Probably not."

"What's your plan?"

"I don't have one. I called you. You picked me up. Now I'm here."

"You need a plan."

"I know."

"Well let's think of one."

"It's not that easy."

"Try."

"Okay. Just spit balling here. How's this. I lay low here a few days. I should be safe. No one knows you exist. I always tell people I'm an only child. And that my parents are dead. Sorry, about that. No offense—it's just we haven't spoken in ten years. Then I use the convenience of us being twins to travel to the Caribbean using your passport. Don't worry, I'll send it back to you. Or you can just report it lost or stolen or something. And then I'll settle down at some resort somewhere. A real swanky place. Get a job bartending at one of those beachside cabanas. Make Piña Coladas and Daiquiris all day. Then marry some rich middle-aged divorced woman and live happily ever after."

"That's not a plan," Liam says.

"It's something."

"It sounds like a bad movie."

"Part of it is a bad movie plot, I think. From the eighties. *Cocktail* with Tom Cruise."

"Victor. You call me up, ask for my help, and then get here and act like a…like a…"

"Like a what?"

"You're just acting way too casual about all this."

"Maybe it's because I feel like I'm losing my mind."

"And what was the deal with eating all that stuff?"

"Look. I get it. I'm not acting right. But I do appreciate your help. And I need your help. And I know it's been a long time since we've talked. Since we got along. And that's probably my fault. And I know you're sticking your neck out for me, putting yourself at risk, putting yourself in danger—by helping me. So thank you. I'm grateful. I just need—I just need some time. Some time to think. To get my head straight. To figure this out. Let's just get home. And then we can talk about it. Okay?"

"Okay. Fine. Okay. But Victor..."

"Yeah?"

"I'm glad you're home too. I love you, brother."

"Yeah. I love you too."

"I'm going to pray about this now," Liam says as he grabs the crucifix around his neck.

"You do that," I say. "I'm going to lay back here and digest. And do me a favor—pray that I don't puke, okay? And hey—you mind turning the radio back-on?" Liam looks back at me and shakes his head and smiles in the rearview. Then flips it on: "Alright, we've got Wally from Worcester on the line. He wants to talk about the defense. Go ahead Wally, you're on the air..."

∞

five

We drive into Lawrence. The Merrimack River is partially frozen, giving our already rundown city an even harsher look. I get a pang in my chest as we exit off Route 495 onto South Broadway—returning to a past I hate, but a place I can't escape. A national news profile once called Lawrence, "The City of the Damned." And it's true, it's a place of corruption, poverty, drugs, and violence. But it's also my home. And despite what people say about it—it's a place of diversity and dreams, where culture bubbles up from the cracks in the streets. So sure, there's trash, and tenements, and abandoned textile mills. But there's also beauty. Profound hope in the struggle—in the cultures, in the creativity, in the dreams of the people. I love my home—despite hating to return, despite wanting to leave already. It's like Pap always said, "you are this city—no matter how far you run, it'll always be your home."

"Liam, Liam, pull over," I yell from the backseat.

"What? Why?"

"I want to grab a couple bottles."

"Do you think you should be drinking at a time like this?"

"Just pull over."

"Fine." Liam turns into Sullivan's Liquors. The green sign on the outside with Shamrocks and white lettering is the same as it's always been. Nothing has changed inside either. Everything is just older. More faded and worn. Including Mr. Sullivan, who is miraculously still alive and working the counter. I buy two bottles of Old Grandad Bourbon just like Pap used to get and hop back in the van. We ride down into the neighborhood. Down Jefferson Street. Onto South Bowdoin. Through rows of dilapidated post-WWII tract houses, and into the driveway of our white cape house with black shutters—home.

Once Mom got sick and Liam moved her into the nursing home, I wanted to sell the house and split the dough between us. But Liam insisted we hold onto it. In case Mom got better—but that was never going to happen. So here the house sits. And luckily for me, Liam still pays the utilities on the place, so the lights and heat still work.

I collapse across the couch in the living room and Liam plops down in Pap's cracked leather recliner. Everything is brown. The couch, the chair, the carpeting, the coffee table, the paneled walls—all brown. There is dust and stains allover. The spot where Patches took that dump on the carpet after Mom kicked him is still visible.

The evening news barks at us from the ancient TV. Picture blurred and grainy. No cable. Just old rabbit ear antennas. I sip the bourbon straight from the bottle. I'm trying to get drunk, but it's tough with so much in my stomach. Three-quarters through the first bottle, I'm buzzed and restless. I stagger to my feet and flip off the TV.

"Hey! I was watching that," Liam says.

"With your eyes closed?"

"No, I was watching it."

"You were falling asleep."

"No, I wasn't."

"There's nothing but trash on anyway," I say and pick up Pap's old guitar from its stand next to his chair. The guitar and chair were our memorials to Pap. Mom tried to pawn them both, but me and Liam fought her on it. Took quite a beating for it too. "Here—play something," I say handing the guitar to Liam.

"I'm so out of practice."

"It doesn't matter. I just want to hear you sing anyways."

"I'm tired. I'll sound awful."

"Still better than me. Remember Mom said I had the voice of a slaughtered pig."

"Yeah. She did. Didn't she."

"So come on! Please.

"Fine, fine." Liam grabs the guitar from me and begins to tune it. I've always been jealous of Liam's musical abilities. He inherited Pap's singing voice and guitar skills. They seemed wasted on him. I would have been famous with his talent. Instead, he's singing "Amazing Grace" to old ladies at Sunday Mass.

"What do you want me to play?" Liam asks.

"One of those Irish folk songs. Like Pap used to play."

"I might not remember the words."

"Just make them up. I won't know the difference." I drain the rest of the first bottle of bourbon and start on the second. Liam sings "The Parting Glass." His voice is angelic. Puts me at ease. This is the closest we've been—physically, emotionally—in years. It feels nice, it feels right. It's amazing to watch him—an identical version of me, a better version of me. But in this moment, there is no jealousy. Only admiration, only love. I know he's playing these songs for me. To calm me. To take care of me. To bring Pap back to life. Their voices are so similar. If I close my eyes, and still my mind long enough, I swear that Pap is here. That he's sitting right beside me now—singing: "*so fill to me the parting glass... good night and joy be with you all.*"

∞

six

I finish the second bottle in silence. Liam is asleep in the chair with the guitar on his lap. My mind is racing. What to do, where to go, how to survive. I get up to take a pee. The room spins. I step and stagger. The room spins faster. I take another step. Stumble. Fall. Gag. Vomit fills my cheeks. I cover my mouth and tumble towards the bathroom. I make it through the door, but can't reach the toilet. I puke on the floor—bourbon and sauce and rice and big chunks of chicken. I crawl to the toilet. Wretch. Rest my head on the bowl. A hand touches my shoulder. "Victor. What happened? Are you okay?" Liam asks.

I moan.

"Just relax. I'll take care of it." Liam rubs my back. I throw up more.

When my stomach is empty, Liam hands me a towel. "Let's clean you up," he says and helps me to my feet. "I'm drunk," I slur. Liam helps me strip off my clothes and get into the shower. Water runs down my back. Steam. Head against the wall. Warmth all over. "I'll be right back," he says, "I'm going to get you a towel and some fresh clothes. Are you going to be okay?" I grunt and nod and concentrate on breathing—counting my breaths, trying to overcome the nausea.

Liam returns. He turns off the water and towels me off. I start laughing.

"What's so funny?" he asks.

It's hard to form the words. I murmur and stammer. "I'm ashamed. It's absurd. I'm a grown man. It's absurd. Standing here drunk. Wet. Naked. It's absurd. In front of my own brother. Absurd."

Liam laughs.

"What's so funny?" I slur.

"It is absurd. But I owe you—for all those years." Liam steadies me. I step into a pair of sweatpants. And with vomit still all over the floor, I slip and nearly fall into my own mess. But Liam catches me and pulls me up. "Come on. Let's get you to bed," he says.

"No. No. I need to clean up," I yell.

"Don't worry about it. I got it. Let's get you into bed."

"No. No. I need to clean up," I yell again. And then stumble out into the hall and across to the linen closet. Pull out a stack of towels and a bottle of spray cleaner. Back in the bathroom, I drop onto my knees right into the spew. I start spraying the cleaner and rubbing towels all around, smearing mess across the tiles.

Liam grabs me by the shoulders, "Victor, Victor. I got it. Come on. Leave it."

"No. No. I need to clean up," I keep saying.

"Come on, come on. Leave it."

I'm determined to clean up my own filth. I stumble around the toilet—spraying and swiping and wiping. Liam stands guard—steadying me as I waddle, but it's no use, the bathroom remains a mess. Liam slings his arm under my shoulders and leads me down the hall. Our room is the same as it was in high school. Like flipping on the lights to the past. I collapse across the bottom bunk and stay awake just long enough to see Liam put a glass of water on the bedside table. Then pass out.

∞

seven

I gasp. Awake. Forget where I am. Panic. Pitch dark. The bedside clock says two. No sight or sound of Liam. Alone. I struggle for water. Reach for the bedside table. Take a few sips. Lay back down. Pain. Frantic images flash through my head. Fear pulses in my chest. Terror. Noah and Boris. All the damage I've done. Ashamed of the past—afraid of the future. Mind looping out of control—thoughts jumping and surging like an erratic charge—a million broken pieces exploding out. I'm losing my mind. Unraveling.

I try to collect myself. Be rational. Concentrate. Breathe. But I can't steady my mind. I am panicking. Pulsing. Going insane. This must be what it's like. To lose your mind. This is it. I'm losing it. I've lost it. I'm gone. Lost. Rocking back and forth on the bed. Stuck on the word: 'lost.' Repeating it. Whispering it. Over and over. Rocking back and forth. Back and forth. Stuck on it: 'Lost…Lost…Lost…'

A wild ride. Witnessing my own demise. Laying here. Holding on by a thread. Still aware. But barely. Grasping. Looking for a way to hold on. Frenzied. I start playing with the word: 'Lost…Lost…Lost.' Rolling it around my mouth. Dancing it across my tongue. Thinking: If I change one letter of the word 'lost' it becomes 'cost.' If I change one letter of the word 'cost' it becomes 'coat.' If I change one letter of the word 'coat' it becomes 'moat.' 'Moat' to 'boat.' 'Boat' to 'boot.' 'Boot' to 'loot.' 'Loot' to 'lost.' And I'm back again. 'Lost…Lost…Lost.' But I try again. Continuing on like this. Using this children's game—one that I used to play with Mom of all people—to hold onto my sanity. Turning letters over into new words again and again. Until somewhere in the scattered depths of all this, my breath relaxes, my chest releases, and I drift off.

∞

eight

Still dark—I wake up wet. Sweatpants soaked. Sheets damp. And it takes me a second to realize. I've pissed my pants. I stumble to my feet. Still unsteady. More sober, but weak from all that throwing up. I stagger out into the hallway—legs cramped. Still no signs of Liam. But the bathroom is spotless. He must've scrubbed it. I strip off my soiled sweats and run the bath. Dump in all the shampoo, and watch the bubbles foam. Then I go back to the bedroom for a towel and a change of clothes. Under the glare of the hanging bulb, I see a box of old action figures that I'd stored away years ago. I grab the box.

The bath is filled. Steaming, foaming, bubbling. I empty the box of toys. They plop and splash and disappear under the bubbles. I step in and lower myself slowly. The brace of the hot water is soothing and my exposed body prickles in the cold air. I submerge. Then gather the action figures from the suds and line them up in formation on the edge of the tub. They drip and crackle as bubbles break around them.

A fleeting impulse erupts. It passes—then returns. Takes root. I can't shake it. This thought: I should kill myself. It's simple. No reflection. No deliberation. It feels right. Perfect. I should kill myself. I don't want to be hunted. Don't want to be killed. Don't want to suffer. My life has no meaning or purpose. No future. No love. I should just kill myself and be done. It's clear and reasonable logic. Soothing—because it makes sense. There is a perverse pleasure to the idea. I should kill myself.

I get up from the tub. Walk to the sink—dripping—I rummage through the medicine cabinet. Grab Pap's straight edge shaving razor. We'd kept it as a memento. It's the perfect instrument. I return to the water. Submerge myself again. Bring the blade to my wrist. I inhale.

Think. I'm ready. I press the blade into my flesh. It's still sharp. A pearl of blood forms. I breathe in again. About to swipe—I lock eyes with the actions figures on the edge of the tub. I stop. I can't do it. I can't kill myself. I should. But I can't. So I laugh. And that fortune cookie from earlier pops into my head: *You Must Try—Or Hate Yourself for Not Trying.* And I laugh harder. Because it makes sense now. And because I'm deriving wisdom from a fortune cookie. If I can't kill myself, then I've got to try to survive—to make a life for myself—to find purpose—to make meaning. There's no other option. It's all I can do.

I close my eyes and lay back in the water. Listen to the crackle of the bubbles. I'm smiling. Inspired. I reach out for the action figures—my toys. I start playing with them just like I used to as a kid. Flying, shooting, punching—calling out *pows* and *blams* and *booms* and *wahoos*. Fighting the ultimate battle between good and evil. The fate of the universe in my hands. Splashing and laughing until the war is won. Until justice is done. And then tears. Tears of release. I'm hopeful. And for the first time in a while, I'm almost happy.

∞

nine

One eye open. One eye closed. I lay curled up watching the morning pass through a sliver in the window shade. It's cold, gray. Wind gusting and whistling. A tree branch rustles and scrapes the window. Still no sign of Liam. Still alone. Hungover. Last night like an out-of-body experience, watching someone else. But it was me. Me who ate all that food. Me who drank that booze. Me who threw up. Me who wanted to die. Me who almost killed myself. But didn't. And I'm glad. And I'm going to try. Try to figure it out. Make it better. Try to live.

I get myself together. Wash my face and put on some old clothes from my closet. They're all too tight. But I find some sweats and a jacket that will fit. I search the house for Liam. But he's gone—his van gone from the driveway too. I pick up the phone to call him, but then I remember that I don't know his number, that it's saved in my phone somewhere deep in the Atlantic. I go into the garage. Mom's rusted Oldsmobile sedan is still in there. The keys are on the hook in the wall of the kitchen just like they used to be. The car door whines as I open it. I put the key in the ignition and turn. It stutters for a second, but then turns over and starts up.

There are two things I need to do before I go. One is easy. The other terrifies me.

∞

ten

Pap is buried at the Immaculate Conception Cemetery on top of Tower Hill. His gravestone is twenty paces from the giant American Oak at the apex of the hill. I've counted hundreds of times. Snow has covered the engraving on his stone. I dig it away with my bare hands. The wet cold turns my skin red and raw. It reads: *CARROLL | William Flannery | June 11, 1947 – November 7, 1987 | Loving Husband, Father, and Friend.*

Pap went by Billy. Not a single person ever called him William. Maybe his mother did, but she died before we were born. Pap wasn't a William. He was a Billy. Billy is big, funny, and loving. William is too serious. But Mom insisted that the stone say William. Billy wasn't proper she had said. One day I'm going to have a new stone put in here. One that says Pap's real name. One that says Billy.

"I miss you, Pap," I say out loud. "And it sure would be nice to hear you laugh right now. To go for a ride on your motorcycle. Go fast. And laugh and scream." The wind gusts and howls through the trees. "Is that you, Pap?" I ask turning back to look at the giant oak. The wind dies and the branches go still. "Didn't think so," I say. "Anyways, if by chance you can actually hear me, and if for some reason you have any power or pull out there in the Great Beyond, I sure could use your help. Especially right now. Because I'm in some deep trouble. So yeah. Love you, Pap. And…and…I just wish I could hear you laugh."

∞

eleven

Dry heat blasts my face as I enter St. Ann's Nursing Home. A heat so dry it'll make your skin crack. But it's so cold outside that I'm glad for this burst of hot air. It warms the blood. Makes me shiver. A metallic blue artificial Christmas tree decorated with paper stars and blinking colored lights stands in the lobby. It's surrounded by a pile of tattered presents—their wrappings worn at the edges. I pick up one of the boxes and shake it. Empty. And then another and another. They're all empty. Just props. The paper star ornaments have pictures of the patients pasted on them. Everyone is smiling in their pictures. And yet, the smiles are tragic. Forced. Just like many patients themselves into this nursing home. Placed here by their families against their will—forgotten, ignored, waiting to die.

Mom's ornament hangs from a bottom branch. If it weren't for her startling blue eyes, I wouldn't have recognized her. Her skin so saggy, her hair so thin. And that fixed smile, as artificial as this tree. Yet despite this, I move her picture to a more prominent spot—in the middle, facing the door. And then so her star is not overshadowed, I reposition a few of the surrounding ornaments to more distant branches. It's a point of family pride.

A tired woman with a marshmallow face sits at the front desk. I approach, but she doesn't look up. "Ah. Excuse me. Hello, I'm…" I start to say. But she stops me, sticking her palm out towards my face. She reaches into a box of tissues and blows her nose—a long brass horn blow. Then she rubs her nose raw, crumples the tissue, and throws it on the desk in front of her. It's one of many piled there—a mountain of influenza. Finally, she looks up at me. "Okay, what do you want?"

"Ah, yeah," I say, "I'm here to see my mother. Grace Carroll?"

"Oh my gosh. You're Father Liam's brother. Grace's other son?"

"Um, yes."

"You look just like Father Liam?"

"Well, we're twins, so…"

"What's your name?"

"Victor."

"Victor! That's right, that's right. Your brother told us all about you."

"Nothing but good things, I'm sure," I say. But she ignores this.

"Hey Patty, hey Patty, come out here," she calls into the office doorway behind her.

A thin ghost-like lady emerges. "This is Grace's other son. Father Liam's brother."

"Oh my gosh. The resemblance is striking," she says.

"Well, like I was just saying, that happens with twins sometimes."

The ladies start talking over each other in rapid succession.

"We've heard so much about you."

"So much about you."

"We've been wondering if you'd ever come."

"Yeah, we've been wondering."

"Father Liam's told us all about you."

"All about you."

"What a wonderful man, your bother."

"Such a wonderful man. A saint, really."

"Yes, a saint."

"He's so good with your mother."

"So good."

"Oh gosh, your mom is going to be so happy to see you."

"So happy."

"She's so sweet, your mom."

"Definitely one of our favorites."

"Definitely."

"She's a perfect angel!"

At this, I have to chime in: "My mom? My mom is a perfect angel?"

"An angel!" they both say in unison.

"So, ah, is she available? I mean, can I see her?" I ask.

"Of course, of course," the front desk lady says, "she'd love to see you."

"Yeah, she's right over there, in the activity room," the thin lady says pointing.

"Okay, thanks," I say.

The activity room lacks activity. Smells of decay. A milling herd of wheelchairs gathers around a TV that's blaring the weather channel. Geriatrics struggle to read books with oversized print and play gin rummy with jumbo-sized cards. Trembling hands drag checker and chess pieces across their respective boards. A drooling invalid yells incoherently over the whistling of his hearing aids. What an inglorious way to die.

I spot Mom in the corner. Her blue eyes piercing even from across the room. She is sitting in a wheelchair pushed up against a table where two other women are playing checkers. I walk over to her. She seems incoherent—looks at me without recognition. The checker ladies ignore me too. Her body is a rotting sack of flesh. Her skin, pale and blue and veiny. Her body, hunched and frail.

"Hi, Mom," I say. "It's me, Victor." I lean in and touch her arm. She screams.

"She doesn't like to be touched," shouts one of checker ladies.

"Sorry. I didn't know," I say.

"Yeah, she doesn't like to be touched," the other lady repeats.

"Fine," I say, "but she's my mother."

92

I wheel Mom to her room—stopping at the front desk to ask for directions. Every entryway is locked and requires a security button to be pressed in order to pass through. It prevents patients with dementia from wandering away. But it makes the place feel like a prison. I roll Mom into her room and pull up a chair beside her. It's stifling and sparse—a hospital bed, a small dresser, a wooden chair, and a bedside table with a crucifix, a Bible, and a silver double-picture frame on it. The photos are of me and Liam as kids, and a wedding portrait of Mom and Pap. I assume Liam put these here. I pick up the frame and study Mom and Pap. Mom was beautiful when she was young. And Pap was so handsome. They look so happy. I wonder if Pap knew that she was such a mean drunk when he married her? One thing is for sure, there is absolutely no resemblance between the beautiful woman in this photo and the decomposing one in the wheelchair in front of me.

Mom's eyes glaze—I doubt she has any understanding. I reach out and touch her again. Her gaze snaps into focus. My chest tightens, my throat clenches. That glare—it brings me back to her drunken rages, to her curses, to her wire coat hanger beatings. "I know you!" she screams. "You're that degenerate ding-dong who lives down the street!"

I jump back in my seat.

"Ding-Dong!" she screams again—her eyes rolling back into her head.

"Mom, it's me. It's Victor," I say.

"Ding-Dong!" She screeches—her voice pitched and raspy like a demon.

I try to calm her. Plead with her. But she keeps screaming. Starts stripping off her dress. Exposing her breasts. I turn my head. Keep pleading. But she doesn't stop. I grab the blanket from her bed and throw it over her. She spits in my face. I wipe it away and just stand there. I try shushing her. But that only makes her yell louder. I turn and run out of the room—down the hallway—the sound of Mom's curses echoing behind me.

I duck into an open room—some kind of employee lounge. A refrigerator hums in the corner, a clock ticks on the wall. A long plastic folding table stands in the middle of the room. There's a large sheet cake on it that reads: "Happy Birthday Gabriela." A few slices have already been eaten. I pick up the knife lying beside it and cut off a big corner piece. Then shove the whole thing in my mouth. Buttermilk frosting—my favorite.

"Excuse me! Can I help you?" A voice calls from behind me.

I turn around. An attractive young woman stands in the doorway. Short, curvy, dark hair, beautiful skin. She's wearing medical scrubs. "I'm visiting my mother," I mumble through the cake in my mouth.

"Well, it looks like you're stealing my cake," she says.

"Ah, yeah, sorry, you caught me," I say holding up my frosting covered hands.

"That's my cake!" she yells.

"Really? Awesome! So you're Gabriela? Happy birthday!"

Gabriela shakes her head and smiles. "What are you doing here?" she asks.

"Visiting my Mom. Grace…Grace Carroll."

"Now I know why you look familiar. You're Father Liam's brother?"

"That's me."

"I've never seen you here before. Your brother's always here. But I've never seen you."

"Victor. My name is Victor."

"Okay, Victor. How come you never come to visit your mother?"

"I live far away, and well…I hate my mother."

"Your mom is a sweetheart. What are you talking about?"

"A sweetheart? How's this for sweet?" I say, then turn around and lift my shift, exposing the scars on my back. "You see these? These are from her. Used to beat us like race horses. Liam's got them too. I bet he never mentioned that to anyone around here. So you tell me, you still think my mother's a sweetheart?" I lower my shirt and turn back around. Gabriela says nothing. I feel exposed—like a bug pinned to a wall. I shouldn't have shown her the scars.

"I'm sorry," she says, "I had no idea."

"Don't worry about it. It was years ago."

"But still…"

"Actually, can you help me?" I ask to change the subject. "I was just in my mom's room, and I left because she started screaming and swearing at me, and I didn't know what to do. That's why I came in here. I just needed to get away."

"Oh that. She does that sometimes."

"She does that 'sometimes.' You say that so casually."

"It's the Alzheimer disease. It's a mean disease. Fits like that are not uncommon."

"Really?"

"Here. Come on," she says, "we'll go settle her together. You'll see."

We enter Mom's room. She's still muttering obscenities. Gabriela goes to her, pulls up her dress, and covers her with the blanket. "There you are, Grace. That's much better," she says.

"Shut up, ding-dong," Mom yells. I burst out laughing—the sadness and the absurdity overwhelm me. But Gabriela takes the insult in stride. She caresses Mom's hand and responds in a sweet tone, "No. You shut up, ding-dong." I stutter in disbelief, and Mom screams back, "Shut up, ding-dong!" So again, Gabriela says sweetly, "No. You shut up." Then turns to me and whispers, "Just wait."

"Shut up, ding-dong," Mom shouts.

"No, you shut up, ding-dong," Gabriela says.

"Ding-Dong," Mom says in a calmer tone.

"Ding-Dong," Gabriela repeats.

"Ding-Dong," Mom says.

"Ding-Dong," Gabriela repeats.

"Ding-Dong," Mom whispers.

"Ding-Dong," Gabriela whispers back.

"Ding-Dong," Mom mumbles.

"Ding-Dong," Gabriela echoes.

"Ding-Dong," Mom murmurs.

"Ding-Dong," Gabriela echoes.

Mom sighs. Quiet. Not asleep. But still. Her eyes glaze over. She's far away—gone. Gabriela strokes her hand and puts a pillow behind her neck. Then she turns to me, sits down on the bed, and pats the spot beside her inviting me to sit.

"What was that?" I whisper.

"Dementia."

"Yeah, but…but, how'd you do that?"

"Funny thing. One day, a while back, I got so pissed off at her when she was screaming at me, that I screamed back. And she liked it. Made her quiet. So I started doing it. Works every time. No idea why. But it works."

"That's amazing," I say, staring at her in admiration.

"Now. You sit here and visit with your mother in peace," she says, standing to leave.

"Wait," I say, "what am I supposed to do?"

"Talk to her, silly."

"About what?"

"Here," she says, grabbing the Bible off the bedside table and handing it me. "Read to her. She likes it when you read to her. It always works for your brother." And then she turns to go.

"Wait."

"What?"

"What...ah...what part? I mean what part do I read to her?"

"Try the Proverbs," she says. "She seems to like those." Then she turns again to go.

"Wait, wait!"

"Yes?

"Um...ah...Happy Birthday. And thanks. Thank you."

"Thanks. And you're welcome. And you'll be fine. Just talk to her," she says and leaves.

Mom's eyes are cloudy. Her head slouched. Her mouth ajar. A bit of spittle hangs from the corner of her mouth. I put the Bible down, lean into her, take the corner of her blanket, and use it to wipe the spittle from her mouth. She doesn't seem to mind my touch this time. So I stand up, gently take her head in my hands and straighten her neck. I sit back down and pick up the Bible.

"Well, Mom, I can honestly say that sitting here alone with you— you in a wheelchair, me with a Bible in my hands—is not an image I ever thought possible. But here we are. If only Liam could see us now. I bet he'd love this. To be honest though, I'm not sure why I'm even here— why I came. I felt like I needed to, I guess. But now that I'm here, I not sure what to say. I mean I'm not sure there is anything to say. And if there was, you wouldn't understand me anyways. Would you?"

I pause. I don't expect Mom to comprehend. But I stop anyways. Just in case.

"Seeing you here now. Like this. It's sad. It's just sad. Part of me wishes you had just drunk yourself to death a long time ago. You would have been happier that way. I would have been happier. It would've been easier to hate you. Because now I can't hate you. Not anymore. Not like this. I can't. And I'm not angry either. Now, don't get me wrong, I'm not going to forgive you. I'll never forgive you. For what you did. For what you did to us. That's something I can't ever forgive. Maybe Liam can. But I can't. None of this really matters anyway. You're demented and I'm a dead man. We're both headed to the grave. And I may even beat you there."

Mom closes her eyes. Falls asleep. I take her hand in mine and hold it. I flip through the Bible with the other. Find the Proverbs. And begin to read out loud: *"The beginning of Wisdom is this: Get Wisdom. Though it may cost all you have, get understanding. Cherish Wisdom, and she will exalt you; embrace her, and she will honor you..."*

∞

twelve

The bells of Saint Francis Church are ringing—calling out to worshippers from two looming gothic spires. I walk up the church's granite steps, through its arched double doors, and into one of the pews in back. I'm overcome with nostalgia. This is who I am. This place. These people. This city. I am from here—this stack of red bricks. I'm from altar boys who snack on Eucharist, who steal Holy Wine, who sniff funeral incense, who cut class in Confessionals. I'm from the school down the road run by the Sisters of Notre Dame. I'm from their holy smacks and ruler strikes across my open palm. I'm from poems and prayers memorized, written, and repeated by rote—I'm from no math and no science, but I know, "a sentence is a group of words expressing a complete thought" because I've said it so many times. I'm from parochial playgrounds—from four square games and dodge ball and tackle football on pavement. I'm from the boy's side and the girl's side, and leave room for the Holy Ghost. I'm from plaid skirts rolled-up too short and unexpected boners in math class. I'm from hot lunch lines—from mashed potatoes served from ice cream scoops, from ham and bean suppers, and cardboard pizza on Fridays. I'm from, "Think of all that Jesus accomplished by thirty-three, what will you have accomplished by then?" It's the very question that got me started on this journey. Where I developed my desire for fame—my desire to escape this place. And yet, here I am. Full circle. Back where I began. Hidden in a pew under the shadows of the organ balcony. The prodigal brother returned.

Liam stands on the altar saying Mass. It never gets any less surreal to see him in robes—my own twin brother as a priest. When it's time for Communion, I get in Liam's line—keeping my head bowed, trying to avoid attention. When it's my turn, and he sees me, instead of the usual "Body of Christ" that he is supposed to say, he hisses at me in a whisper, "What are you doing here?"

"I wanted to surprise you," I whisper back.

"Where have you been? I went to the house. You were gone."

"I went out."

"I've been trying to call you?"

"No phone."

"You shouldn't be here. People will see you. Go. Now," he says loudly, causing the folks around us to turn and stare. So I duck my head, turn back down the aisle, and head straight out of the church.

∞

thirteen

Back at home, Liam bursts into the kitchen.

"What the hell were you thinking showing up like that?" he yells.

"I thought it would be nice. To see you saying Mass."

"You know how many people saw you? Recognized you?"

"I was sitting in the back."

"You know the cops called the rectory this morning? Thank God I was saying Mass and Father Donahue intercepted the call. Gave me time to think. You know what they were calling about? You! That's right, you! Father Donahue said that they were asking all sorts of questions about you. You, Victor, you. That guy you're in trouble with…"

"Noah."

"Yeah well, he has connections. And he's on to you. I don't know how he knows that you're here, but he knows. And you're in trouble. Big trouble. I mean, if he has the power to be sending local cops after you—God Almighty—you're in big, big, trouble."

"I know," I say.

"And then you have the gall to show up at church like that."

"No!" I yell. "No. No. No!"

"What?" Liam asks.

"The bourbon I bought yesterday. I paid with my credit card! That's how Noah tracked me. That must be it. That's the only way he could know. My credit card. I ditched my phone. Bought my bus ticket with cash. But I used my stupid credit card for the booze. It's the only way."

"Well, I'll be darned, that's impressive," Liam says.

"Really? That's your response?"

There is a knock at the door. We freeze.

"Hide," Liam says. "In the ghost spot. Go. Now."

I scurry behind the door to the basement. Sit on the top step and peer through a crack. Liam approaches the front door, turns back to be sure I'm clear, then opens it. It's the cops. I can see the blue of their uniforms.

"Evening, Miguel. Evening, Tommy. What can I do for you?" Liam asks.

"Evening Father Carroll. We are hoping you can help us."

"Well boys, I'm always willing to help some fellow parishioners."

"We're looking for your brother, Victor. We're hoping you can help us locate him."

"Well, I'm afraid, I haven't seen my brother for a very long time. We had a falling out some time ago. It's been years since I've seen him. Years since he's been home. To be honest, he's somewhat of a lost sheep."

"No offense, Father, but we got reports that he attended your Mass at Saint Francis just a couple hours ago. And we've also got witnesses who say he was at your mother's nursing home today too."

"Well, gosh darn boys, this is all news to me. Can I ask what this is all about?"

"Not sure exactly. But we got a call at the station this morning from some of the big wigs down in Boston. Word is that some important folks are looking for him. Not sure what he did, but he's wanted in New York for questioning in some big case."

"Sounds serious."

"Definitely. We were told to make finding him our number one priority."

"Well, boys, like I said, I haven't seen him, or heard from him in a long time."

"You wouldn't mind if we took a look around in the house for him then, would you?"

"Fellas, I'm your pastor. You don't believe me?"

"Sorry, Father. It's not that we don't believe you. It's just…well… our job."

"Sure. Sure. I understand. Come on in then."

I jump to my feet. Move as fast as I can down the basement steps. Every creak makes my heart race faster. I run to the furnace. Slide on my knees. Remove the metal ventilation covering and squeeze into the hidden space behind it. This is the 'ghost spot.' For about a year when we were younger, I convinced Liam that our house was haunted. He didn't know about this crawl space. I used to hide here and howl. Make him think there was a ghost.

One of the cops comes down into the basement. Walks all around. Comes up to the furnace. Knocks on it. Bends down. Shines a light under it. I didn't have time to replace the ventilation cover. He extends his flashlight towards the crawl space. He's so close that I can hear him breathe. If he listens hard enough, he'd be able to hear my heart pounding. I hear him drop on his belly and start to crawl towards me.

The furnace kicks on with a loud clank. The cop startles. Bangs his head. "Goddamnit!" he cries. The furnace burns and hisses. The cop backs himself up onto his feet then plods up the stairs. I'm safe. Still, I don't dare move until Liam comes down and tells me it's clear.

We sit on the bottom basement step under the glare of a bare hanging bulb. Liam has covered the two small foundation windows with cardboard so that no one can see inside. The rest of the house sits in darkness. For a long while, we do not speak. Just silence—listening for signs of anyone creeping around the house.

"We need a plan," Liam whispers.

"I know," I say, "but all I keep coming back to is that stupid idea I had earlier. Where I go to Mexico or the Caribbean or someplace. Buy a ticket with cash. Use your passport to get there. Then mail it back to you. Or you just report it lost or stolen. And I'll hide out there until things cool off. Get some under-the-table bartending job or something. Or you can loan me some cash if you got it. Figure out the rest later. But it's dumb right? Would never work?"

"No, not necessarily," Liam says as he stands and turns up the steps.

"What do you mean?"

"Maybe not if you went far enough way."

"Like where?"

"I've got an idea. Just sit tight here. I'll be back."

"Where are you going?"

"No time to explain. Just stay here. Don't leave the basement until I get back."

"Come on. Just tell me."

"Just stay here. Promise?"

"Liam?"

"Promise?"

"Yeah, I promise."

"I'll be back as soon as I can," he says and leaves up the stairs.

The rest of the night is a blur. I have no phone and there is no clock down here, so I've got no sense of time. I pace around the basement alone with my thoughts. I feel like Jack Torrance from *The Shining* losing my mind and waiting for the furnace to explode. All I want to do is escape. To start over. Get a second chance. I keep thinking about how I truly wanted, needed, to die last night. And yet, here I am now—desperate to survive.

Liam returns at dawn. Pale light creeps through the cracks between the cardboard and the window. He comes down into the basement and throws me of set of clothes. "Here, put these on."

"What's this?"

"Clerical clothes. I have a collar for you in the car. You'll need them to travel."

"Where am I going? What's going on?"

"I'll explain later. Hurry up and change. And let's go."

I scramble into the black clerical clothes. They're tight. Liam is thinner than me. Doesn't indulge as much as me. But I suck in my gut and make them fit. At the top of the stairs, Liam turns to me. "Crawl," he says.

"What?"

"Crawl behind me until we get into the garage. Someone is outside watching us."

I drop to all fours and follow him through the kitchen and out into the garage.

"Okay, now lay across the back of the van. I grabbed a bunch of donation blankets from church. I'll bury you under them. If the cops pull me over for some reason, to question me or something, at least these may hide you."

"Are you going to tell me the plan now?"

"No time, just get in."

The garage door opens and we drive. Morning light shines through the blankets.

"Tell me what's going on," I say to Liam.

"Can't talk. We're being followed. I have a plan."

We drive in silence. I listen to the hum of the tires. Try to guess where we're going using sound and speed and the bumps in the road. But it's useless. So I'm left to lay still—confused and afraid—my fate entirely in Liam's hands.

A garage door opens. I wonder if we are back home again. Unable to shake our tail.

"Wait here. I'll be right back."

"Where are we?"

"Just wait here."

Time ticks by. I have nothing to do but count my breaths. Helpless.

The car door opens. Liam pulls off the blankets. We're not at home—somewhere else. "Okay, let's go," he says. I crawl out of the van and struggle to my feet. An old man is standing there. Another priest. He's big and round with a white beard—looks like Santa Claus. "Victor, meet Father Donahue. Father Donahue, meet my brother Victor." We shake hands. Turns out we're inside the rectory garage. "Father Donahue has agreed to help us," Liam says, "I didn't explain everything. But I explained enough. I can't drive anywhere without being followed. So we're both going to duck in the back of his car and he'll drive us."

"Where? Where is he driving us?"

"To the airport. Well, actually just outside it. To East Boston. I know a safe spot to leave you. From there, you'll take a cab to Logan. We can't risk getting seen while dropping you off. I'll explain the rest when we get there. For now, we need to move."

"But what's the plan? You haven't told me the plan yet."

"This is the plan. It's happening now. You have to trust me. Okay?"

"Okay," I say.

Liam opens the back of his van and starts pulling out a canvas duffel bag. I recognize it immediately. It's Pap's army bag. From when he served in Vietnam. "Put this in Father Donahue's trunk. I'll grab the blankets. I packed you all the clothes you'll need. They're all mine, so you probably won't like them—and you're going to have to lose some weight."

"Hey!"

"Just saying."

"This thing is heavy," I say lifting the bag.

"I put in a few stacks of Bibles. And a couple boxes of Rosary Beads. It's good cover."

"Can we take out some of the Bibles?"

"Just keep them. You might need them."

"You boys about ready?" Father Donahue asks.

I look at Liam. "Let's do it," I say and he nods. We crawl into the back of Father Donahue's Lincoln. I lay on the floor and Liam lays on the seat. Father Donahue covers us with blankets. It feels almost like our bunk beds back at home. Reminds me of when we use to make pillow forts out of sheets and couch cushions. The garage door opens and we roll out of the rectory.

"You see that gray Chevy Malibu parked on the street?" Liam asks.

"I do," Father Donahue responds.

"Let me know if it follows us."

We drive a few blocks.

"All clear," Father Donahue says, "I think they're still sitting at the rectory.

"Can we sit up?" I ask.

"Let's stay down just in case," Liam says.

Thirty minutes later, Father Donahue is idling in his car, while Liam and I stand beneath a thirty-two-foot-tall statue of the Virgin Mary. We're at the Mary, Queen of the Universe, Shrine in the Orient Heights neighborhood of East Boston. We used to come here as teenagers to get high. This is where Liam had his awakening—his calling to God. I was hooking up with Meghan McDonald in the back seat of our car, while Liam was having an epiphany about the nature of heaven and hell.

"So, what's the deal?" I ask him plainly.

"As of three hours ago, there were six tickets left on the Delta flight to South Africa. Three hours to Atlanta. Sixteen to Johannesburg.

I make the flight a couple of times a year as a volunteer. I do mission work there. I know a nun there. Mum Mary is her name. She runs an orphanage. And does palliative care for HIV patients. She's a good friend of mine. We've been through thick-and-thin together. She's a total badass. Back during the Apartheid days, she used to smuggle guns and hide freedom fighters for the ANC—for Nelson Mandela's people. So I called her. I didn't tell her any details—she didn't want to know. I told her it's an emergency. That I'd vouch for you—you're my brother after all. And she agreed to safehouse you. To let you hide out there. Live with her. Work at the orphanage. At her place. No questions asked."

"Jeez—I don't know what to say."

"Don't say anything. Just listen," he says and takes an envelope from his pocket. "Take this. It's just over seven grand. After you buy your ticket, you'll have about five left. It's not a ton. But where you'll be living—and with the exchange rate—it'll last you a while. Also, here's my passport and license. I've got a volunteer visa in there already. It all checks out. Oh, and give me your wallet. You can't take your credit cards. Don't want you messing up and using them again by accident."

"Oh come on, I…"

"Just give them to me."

I hand him my wallet.

"Now…"

"Where'd you get the money from?" I cut him off and ask.

"I took it from the Church safe."

"You shouldn't have done that. I don't want you getting in trouble."

"For helping you? Pretty sure I'm already aiding and abetting. Taking the Church's cash reserve from the safe is the cherry on top. Besides, I'm the one responsible for the cash. I'll just replace it with my own savings from the bank. Take out a little at a time, so no one gets suspicious."

"And what about Father Donahue?"

"What about him?"

"Why are you so certain he's not just going to rat us out?"

"Because Father Donahue has secrets too."

"What do you mean?"

"I mean that he's no angel either."

"You mean, like, little boys and stuff?"

"Oh gosh, no, no—nothing like that. Mrs. McNamara. One our parishioners. She's a widower. They've been going at it for years since her husband died. She practically gives him a casserole every night of the week."

"I hope that's not an innuendo."

"Stop it."

"Anyways," I say, "I don't know how to ever repay you for helping me. And I'm sorry. For everything. I went to see Pap yesterday. And to the nursing home to see Mom too. She looks awful. I don't know how you decided to forgive her. But thanks. Thanks for taking care of her. Thanks—for taking care of me. I love you."

"I love you too."

We hug—a deep, long, suffocating squeeze.

"Your cab will be here any minute. We should go."

"Yeah."

"Oh, shoot. One more thing," Liam says, "your collar." He removes the stiff, white clerical collar he's wearing around his neck and tucks it into my shirt. It's so tight that it makes swallowing difficult. Liam laughs at this. "Be safe," he says. "I'll be praying for you."

"I will. And I'll need it."

We hug once more. Give each other a last look. Then Liam slides back into the backseat of Father Donahue's Lincoln, covers himself in blankets, and he's gone. I'm left standing there under a thirty-two-foot tall statue of the Virgin Mary. I'm an atheist. And I haven't prayed since Pap died. But I get down on my knees, close my eyes, and recite a 'Hail Mary.' And I keep saying them—right up until the cab arrives. It seems right.

∞

fourteen

I buy my ticket, go through security, and board the plane—looking over my shoulder constantly, expecting Boris or the cops to be there, waiting for them to snatch me and thwart my escape. But that moment never arrives. It is hard to be inconspicuous dressed as a priest. People stare at you. One little old lady even comes up to me and asks for a blessing. I oblige by putting my hands on her shoulder and praying an 'Our Father.'

Once I'm in my seat, I breathe a sigh of relief, and relax enough to steady my nerves and collect my thoughts. I'm headed to South Africa. To live at an orphanage with a nun. I've hopefully just escaped being murdered and having my organs sold on the black market in China. I've got about five grand in cash, an uncertain future, and almost twenty hours of flight time to figure it all out. I'll be arriving at night in Johannesburg, so I'll need to find a place to stay. Then Liam said it's about a six-hour drive to Mum's Mary orphanage. So I'll need to figure out a way to get there. And I'll need to exchange money, get a new phone, and find a way to tell Liam I'm safe. But for right now, I'm exhausted, and all I think about is sleep.

∞

fifteen

I'm thirty-nine thousand feet in the sky, sitting in a tin can, headed for Johannesburg. I slept for three hours on the flight to Atlanta. But now I'm wide awake with sixteen hours to go. Nine hundred-and-sixty-minutes staring at the "FASTEN SEAT BELT WHILE SEATED" sign on the seat in front of me. Over fifty-seven thousand seconds crammed into the middle seat of a seven-forty-seven. It's embarrassing how long it took me to scribble out the math on those minutes and seconds on the back cover of the inflight magazine. But at least it killed a little time. I know we had to move fast, but I wish Liam had packed me a book—something besides the Bible. I'm not one for in-flight movies either. There is something about the little screens and the little seats. It's an injustice to the movies and to passengers, and so I can't concentrate. But beer and booze are free on international flights. So drinking helps pass the time. And with hours and hours to go, I turn to the part-time friends beside me and make idle chatter.

To my right at the window is Dr. Peter Walters, a dentist and big-game trophy hunter from Texas. "I don't like golf, so I hunt instead," he tells me. He's dressed in khaki safari gear—all ready for the hunt—and he looks exactly like what you would expect a trophy hunting dentist from Texas to look like: fat, balding, thick glasses, sun burned skin, and perfect teeth. "I'm going to a hunt a lion," he says, then shows me a bunch of photos of him holding up the carcasses of previous kills—a moose, a bear, a buffalo, a leopard.

"Did you eat all that stuff?" I ask.

"Nope. Had them all stuffed. You should see my house."

"I can only imagine."

"I've been waiting on a lion for years. But the permits are a fortune."

"How much?"

"It's going to cost me fifty grand just for the hunt. Not to mention the import and export costs. Those'll run you another five grand. And then they stick you with a ten grand trophy fee, which is just a killing tax. But it's all worth it, you know, to bag a lion."

"Seems like it would be much easier to just go to a zoo and look at one instead."

"It's not about seeing. It's about being in the wild. It's about the thrill of the kill."

"How does it work? Tracking and killing them?"

"Well from what I've been told, the guides lure them out by strapping a skinned impala carcass to the hood of our truck, then we sit in cover and wait. Like shooting ducks in a barrel."

At this, I burst out laughing. I've had a handful of drinks and not a lot to eat, so I'm a little sloppier than I'd thought. "So let me get this straight," I say, "you pay a ton of money to lure a lion out into a wide open death trap? And then you just basically shoot it point blank? For what? All so you can show off to your dentist buddies back home? Mount its head in your office? No wonder dentists have such high rates of suicide."

"Well, excuse me," Dr. Walters says, "that's a rude thing to say coming from a priest. No wonder you Catholics have so many problems." And then he huffs and goes back to reading his stack of hunting magazines—aggressively flipping the pages and spreading his elbow out over the arm rest. That conversation is over. I keep forgetting I'm wearing Liam's clerical clothes.

I order another beer. "Okay, Father, but that's going to be your last. I'm not supposed to serve you this much," the flight attendant says. I smile and shrug and turn my attention to the young Mormon missionary next to me on the aisle. He's got a placard pinned on his black suit jacket that says, 'Elder Billows.' He is in the process of writing a letter to his mother. I read over his shoulder. He says he misses her, he prays for her, he loves her. It warms my heart. What a sweet kid. I wonder how my life would've been different if I loved Mom that much? If she wasn't a drunk? If Pap hadn't died? Funny how the pains of the past can sneak up on you when you least expect it.

Elder Billows notices me looking over his shoulder. "I'm writing home," he says.

"Sorry," I say, "I didn't mean be to be nosy."

"That's okay," he says.

"Do me a favor, tell your Dad you love him too. Even if he isn't the emotional type. He'll appreciate it. Trust me," I say and extend my hand. "I'm Victor. Sorry, Liam. My name is Liam. Father Liam Carroll."

"Nice to meet you, Father Carroll. I'm Alex Billows. Would you like a piece of gum?" He shakes my hand—having to awkwardly twist his arm to meet my hand—and then offers me a stick of Juicy Fruit from his pocket.

"Sure," I say and take a piece, "I'll save it for later, if that's okay?"

"Sure. And I hope I'm not being offensive, but you look kind of cramped?"

"What do you mean?"

"In that middle seat?"

"Yeah, it's a bit of a tight fit."

"My friend Tyson is sitting a few rows back on the aisle. He's on his mission too. If you'd like, I'm sure he'd be happy to switch with you. It wouldn't be a problem at all. And then we could sit next to each other."

"Really? He'd want to give up an aisle seat for the middle?"

"Sure. Why not? And if he won't do it, then I'll take the middle. I kind of like it."

"The middle seat?"

"Yes!"

"Why?"

"It's a great place to make friends."

"Well, that's one way of looking at it. Look, I feel bad taking you up on the offer. But honestly, not bad enough to refuse. If you're sincere, then bring it on. Truth be told, I could really use some space to stretch out and get some sleep. I'm exhausted. And I haven't showered in about two days...sorry if I stink by the way."

"I have nothing but respect for all representatives of Jesus Christ."

"Indeed," I say. We make the switch and I soon find myself sitting drunk and relaxed with my legs spread into the aisle. Even better, my new seatmates are a young couple cuddling together watching a movie—so no Dr. Walters jamming his elbow over the armrest either. That Mormon kid sure was sweet. I'm glad I resisted the urge to make magic underwear and polygamy jokes. Anyways, I close my eyes and try to drown out my thoughts. Do my best not to think about the last few days and weeks. Avoid thinking about the future. The unknown. Fear. Regret. Shame. Longing. Desire. Thoughts cycling like the steady drone of the engines churning. Somewhere in there, I drift off to sleep.

∞

sixteen

Passengers scream. I wake up to flashing lights and dangling oxygen masks. A storm is raging outside. The plane rattles violently and free falls from the sky—diving—ripping through clouds and rain and lightning. I reach out, grab my oxygen mask, and breathe deep. I'm calm. It seems strange to feel so calm. But I'm calm. The couple next to me are clutching each other and professing, "I love you, I love you." Dr. Walters is white knuckle gripping the seat in front of him. The two Mormon boys have their heads bowed in prayer. Others are praying as well. Many are crying. I look around and the scene resonates with beauty. I realized that's a twisted thought—to see beauty in this moment. The panic as we plummet. People at their most vulnerable. Coping with peril. Contemplating their fleeting life.

My life should be flashing before my eyes. But it's not—I'm drawing a blank. I try to force the issue. Hold pictures of Pap and Liam—even Mom—in my mind. Grasp onto memories of Marco and Bobby and Jinhee. Even of Noah and Boris. But nothing sticks. None of it seems to matter. Nothing matters. And so as the screams get louder, the panic rises, and the end nears—I am sad. Truly—deeply. Saddened by the meaninglessness of my existence. Time without purpose. Futility. A wasted life. Tears and a handful of dust. This will be my end.

But the plane levels off. The lights return to normal. The screams subside. The cabin steadies. And the pilot comes on the loud speaker, "Ladies and Gentleman, this is your captain speaking. Just wanted to let you know that everything is okay. I repeat, everything is okay. You may remove your emergency oxygen masks now. I apologize about the fright there. As it turns out lightning does strike twice—now usually our systems are set up to handle the static discharge of getting hit by lightning. But getting hit twice like that in rapid succession caused our systems to short out for a second and for us to lose cabin pressure. That's why those lovely masks dropped down for you. As for the rapid decent, I want to assure you that it was controlled. I know it may not have felt like that. But we never lost engine power. FAA regulations require that we make a steep controlled emergency decent to a level where it is possible for all passengers to breathe without the need for those masks. Again, sorry for the fright. But all is well. However, deployment of the oxygen masks requires us to land immediately. And unfortunately, they'll be dangling there for the rest of the flight. There's no retract button. But lucky for us, Johannesburg is our closest airport. So we will actually be landing early. So that's a positive. So sit back, relax, and try to enjoy what I promise will be a gradual decent into Johannesburg's O.R. Tambo International Airport."

People cheer. Strangers hug and high-five. The couple next to me starts making out. Dr. Walters is crying. The Mormon boys are saying prayers of gratitude. And what pops into my mind is that fortune from the General Tso's challenge. *You must try—or hate yourself for not trying.* A silly note inside a stale cookie suddenly rings true to me like the profound wisdom of some mystic sage. I've got a second chance. And I better try to make the most of it.

Part Three

∞

one

South Africa. I've landed. Off the plane. Into a new life. A new adventure. A fresh start. A world apart from home. Unfettered from the perils of my debt. Free from the troubles of my past. I'm safe here. At least for now.

I'm ecstatic. Still buzzing from the storm and turbulence and nose dive. Alive with the energy of this new beginning. What next? I step into the chaos of O.R. Tambo. A loud jarring space—painted white and gray and beige with glaring lights and stale air. A traversing-mass crisscrossing over hard waxy tiles—dragging bags and whining children. The same congested herd of travelers universal to all major metropolitan airports.

I zigzag through the customs and immigration line—dissipating my anxiety by chomping on the piece of gum the Mormon kid gave me. When it's my turn, I approach the kiosk—haphazardly spitting the gum into what's left of the wrapper and sticking it in my pocket—then handing over my immigration form along with Liam's passport and visa.

"Hello," I say to the officer.

"Hello," she says with the flat tone and blank expression of a government official.

"I'm very excited to be here. I had a crazy time getting here."

"Where will you be staying on your trip?"

"Ah, um, I'm volunteering at an orphanage. Doing some mission work there." I fumble with my answer realizing now that I don't actually know where Mum Mary's orphanage is located. Or any South Africa geography for that matter.

"And how long will you be staying?"

"Two weeks, I believe. Yeah, two weeks." I bought a round trip ticket to avoid suspicion, obviously with no plans of returning home any time soon, but I forgot the exact date of the return flight. The immigration officer studies me for a long moment. "Just a moment," she says as she turns and calls to her a supervisor.

"Is there a problem?" I ask.

"Yes," she says.

∞

two

I sit in a cold metal administrative room—escorted here by some not-so-friendly armed security guards in military fatigues. The lights buzz and flicker—shining down a glaring light. My legs bounce up-and-down nervously as I await whatever is coming. And I try to control my breath by staring at the generic and faded safari photos that hang on the walls in dull and broken frames. The door swings open and a stern administrative type women enters followed by…Boris.

"Hello, Boychik!"

"Boris! What are you doing here?"

"What a flight we had, huh? First class was nice…until that incident."

"I thought I heard someone singing out Mariah Carey while we were falling…"

"Yes! Let the record show that even in my last moments I was thinking of Mariah."

"Were you singing, 'All I Want for Christmas is You?'"

"Oh yes! If I was going to die then I wanted to go out with my favorite song."

"How did you find me?"

"Oh come now, Boychik. I told you never to doubt Noah. And Noah is very mad at you. And therefore I am very mad at you too. You know how much fuel has been wasted tracking you down. And money too. I had to pay this nice woman a large sum for her to agree to stop you and let me take you back home," he says—pointing and indicating the administrative official beside him.

"So what now?"

"We fly home…and well you know…" Boris does a cartoonish slice across his throat.

"Wait!" I yell—reaching into my pocket. I pull out the crinkled piece of paper with Mum Mary's number on it. There's gum stuck to it. I pull it apart with the utmost care. Like a specialist defusing a bomb. Then I hand it to the stern lady with Boris. "Please! Call this number. Whatever he gave you—we can give you more. Please this is the number of an important lady. A holy lady," I say, noticing the cross around the woman's neck. "This guy here—he's a devil, he's evil. Please, trust me. Call her, she will explain."

The administrative woman stares at me blankly. She studies me—it feels like she is searching for something behind my eyes. I feel violated by the depth of her gaze—but I do not break it. And I plead silently—this anonymous woman who now holds my fate in her willingness to make a phone call. She turns to Boris and looks at him. He starts blathering about increasing her payment and about the power of Noah. But she only gives him the same blank stare in response. Then she turns her eyes back to me. "Okay…I will call," she says—and just like that, she turns and leaves me and Boris alone in the room.

"Oh, Boychick! This is getting very interesting."

"Yeah…especially if no one is home to answer that call."

"Just so you know…no matter how this moment ends…I will be coming for you!"

"Oh…I know!"

The administrative official comes back in the room and hands me the slip of paper with Mum Mary's number on it. "You are free to go," she says. "And you," she says—indicating Boris, "You wait here. We must talk further."

I don't wait to see what transpires. I am out of that room fast. Boris calls after me, but his voice is muffled as the door closes behind me, and I am escorted out of immigration. A slew of porters and taxi drivers swarm me as I exit. But I dart through them and head straight for the currency exchange. With Boris still on my tail, I obviously need to get out of here. Fast. But I can't go anywhere without money.

Minus the transaction fee, my five grand in dollars exchanges for approximately sixty thousand South African Rand. Now the porters and drivers are really eyeing me, and I wonder what I'm going to do with all this cash. Even with the money in two-hundred banknote denominations, the pure volume of it makes me a target. And I certainly can't open a bank account and give Noah and Boris more trails to follow. So I'm going to have to figure out a way to stash this. But that's for later. Right now, I need to reach Mum Mary and explain—and to thank her for saving me. And to do that, I need a phone. So I jet across the concourse to a telecom shop and buy a basic model, then have the attendant teach me how to load airtime, which allows me to pay for cell service with cash. The whole time, I'm constantly looking over my shoulder expecting to see Boris. My only logic for doing all of this in plain sight is the hope that Boris won't try to kill me in such a public place.

With cash and communication secured, I grab my bags and run through the airport—past a giant promotional display for the upcoming World Cup, through a pair of sliding doors, and out into the night. There's a luxury hotel directly across the street—and I figure I'm safe from Boris if I pay in cash—so I pay two thousand rand for a room—take the elevator, and then close and lock the door to my room with a deep sigh of relief. Hoping I'm safe for now.

I pull the crinkled paper with Mum Mary's number on it out of my pocket again and dial it on my new phone. The line rings and my heart beats with the same nerves I used to have calling up my teenage crush.

A sonorous voice answers with a lyrical, "Hello."

"Mum Mary?"

"Yes. This is she. Hello?"

"This is ah...Victor Carroll. Father Carroll's brother."

"Right, right. It seems that you are causing me trouble already, Mr. Carroll."

"Yeah, about that. I just want to start by saying thank you. I can't explain how much..."

"Yes, yes. That's enough," she says cutting me off. "Pray and thank God—that is enough. I have no need for such flatteries. I am quite busy here on my side. And I most certainly hope your troubles will not be following you here. So now, please inform me, when do you plan on arriving?"

"As soon as possible, it's just that..."

"Very well. Have you arranged transport?"

"No, I need to figure that out."

"Yes, yes. You must. You simply must."

"Do you have any suggestions?"

"No. I do not. That is for you to determine."

"Ah...okay."

"Am I right to presume you will need directions to our location?"

"Yeah, I have no idea how to get there. But listen, I should tell you..."

Mum Mary cuts me off again and proceeds with a set of curt directions. I barely have time to scribble them out. Then she promptly says, "Very well, good-bye," and hangs up before I have a chance to try and explain that Boris is very much still on my tail. I suppose I can just call her back. But she doesn't seem like the type who would appreciate that. I guess Boris is my problem.

I think about calling Liam. I desperately want to hear his voice. But I decide not to call. It's not safe. They must be watching him. So

I unzip Pap's duffel bag and grab Liam's toothbrush—he packed his toiletry bag for me too. I brush each tooth with vigor and focus. Scrub my tongue raw. Then I stand under a scalding hot shower. For nearly an hour. Blanketed in steam. I drop to my knees. Let the water roll down my back. A ritual cleanse.

I go back inside Pap's bag for a fresh set of clothes. Sitting there is a note from Liam and a small package wrapped in tin-foil. The note reads simply, "Be safe. Be well." I unwrap the foil. It's a sandwich—white bread and mayo. A 'Triple White.' Just like we made as kids. And even though it's been sitting warm and soggy in this bag for over a day, I stand there in my towel—still dripping—and eat it. And cry.

∞

three

It's a sleepless night. I toss and turn expecting Boris to knock at my door. And when I do doze off, I jump awake again from nightmares of Boris standing over me—strangling me to death as he whisper-sings Mariah Carey songs like some deranged homicidal lullaby. I thought I had escaped. But now it seems, it's not a matter of if, but when, he will find me. What to do?

I am out early the next morning looking for a ride. Taxi drivers grab and holler at me. But I spot a guy—relaxed and cool—leaning against the hood of his van. Just waiting. He's stylish—jeans, vest, glasses, boots splattered in neon paint. Reminds me of a guy I might come across back in Brooklyn. Makes me look like a schlub in comparison dressed in Liam's too tight khaki shorts and a navy polo shirt. Regardless, I am drawn to him—he puts me at ease.

"Good morning my friend! Can I give you a lift?"

"Please," I say and he helps me load my bag into the van.

"My name is Vusi," he says.

"Nice to meet you Vusi. I'm Victor."

"Where are you from my brother?"

"America."

"Yes, yes, I can hear from your accent. But what part?"

"Um…most recently, New York—Brooklyn…do you know it?

"Of course, of course. I am a painter. An artist. Of course, I know Brooklyn."

"That's great. I used to be an artist. A filmmaker."

"Beautiful my brother. Beautiful."

"Well, not anymore."

"Once an artist always an artist."

"It would be nice if that were true."

"It is, it is! So where can I take you, Victor? Where do you want to go?"

"I haven't eaten yet. How about a local spot? Some place you like?"

"Eish. I'm hungry too. I know the perfect place to graze."

Vusi drives like a mad man—zooming in-and-out of traffic, wailing on his horn, yelling at other drivers, and bopping his head to the music blasting on his radio. Makes Boris seem like a model driver. And speaking of Boris, I find myself looking over my shoulder every minute or so—expecting him to be tailing us. But so far, so good. Then at an exit marked 'Hillbrow,' Vusi swerves off the ramp, whips a turn, jumps the curb, and skids to a halt. "All right. Let's eat," he says.

"That was awesome," I say. Less stressful when you aren't kidnapped, I guess.

We exit the van into a dirt lot hidden in the shadows of the morning. Other taxi vans are parked around us. Trash scatters in the wind. A group of people are gathered around an oil-drum grill where a man turns over slabs of meat with a long two-pronged fork. Beside them an old woman is hunched over two burning cauldrons—one with a white creamy mixture and the other with some kind of tomato stew. Sizzling spice and fat waft through the air. My stomach grumbles. Vusi greets the crowd with hugs and handshakes. They speak excitedly to each other in another language. "Do you speak Zulu, Victor?" Vusi asks me with a laugh.

"I'm afraid not," I respond and smile.

"I will teach you," he says, then walks over to the guy at the grill. He returns with two huge plates of food. "This is a traditional South African Braai. What you call barbeque in America. In Zulu we say 'Shisa Nyama' which means 'burnt meat.'"

"Shisa Nyama," I repeat back.

"Yebo, yes! And that white porridge, it's called 'pap'." It's corn meal. And that sauce. We call that 'Chakalaka'. It's made of tomatoes and beans and onion and garlic. It is too good. My favorite."

"Sounds amazing."

"Like nobody's business!" he says and hands me my plate.

I take a bite. "Delicious," I say.

"See! I told you. Like nobody's business."

I laugh. "Exactly. Like nobody's business!"

"You are a proper South African now."

"Thanks. I appreciate this. A lot."

"Yebo, my brother. Artists must stick together."

"Yeah, so what type of stuff do you paint?"

"Come and I'll show you." Vusi waves me onward and we walk with our food to the edge of the lot. Around the corner on the side of a brick industrial building is a brightly colored mural. A bloody lion draped in the South African flag running for its life. Behind it a group of cartoonish hunters take aim with rifles.

"Wow. You did that?"

"Yebo, I did."

"It's beautiful."

"The lion is our people. The people of the South Africa. And the hunters are our political leaders. The corrupt ones—ruining our country. Stealing from the poor. Making themselves rich and fat."

"Sounds like the leaders of America too."

"The same but different."

"The same but different indeed."

We finish our food in silence—watching the morning light break across the mural.

"Vusi, let me ask you a favor."

"Sure, sure."

"Do you know a place where I can rent a car? For long term? For cheap?"

"I know a guy. He is a friend. He will hire you one."

"Listen—I'm kind of in some trouble. So I can only pay with cash."

"Sure, sure. I know trouble. I understand. He will do it. This guy. We will make a plan."

We drive further into Hillbrow. Surrounded by urban decay: crumbling buildings, graffitied walls, soot covered windows, laundry hanging from balconies, and streets overflowing with garbage. Crowds of people. Pigeons. Stray dogs. A dead cat rotting in a gutter. The smell of burning rubbish. We pull into a small car lot secured by a high fence and barbed wire. A tall skinny man dressed in a grease-stained white undershirt and jeans comes outside of the garage and greets us. He and Vusi exchange pleasantries in Zulu.

"Stay here. Look around. I have some business to take care of with my friend. But we will work out a deal for you to hire a car. I'll be back," Vusi says then disappears with the owner into the garage office. I roam the lot and survey my options. Lots of rust and dents—a bunch of jalopies. I need something cheap and affordable. But not something that's going to explode and kill me.

Then I see it. A beat-up motorcycle by the entryway. A Honda touring bike with storage pods on the sides and back, just like the one Pap used to have. I swing my leg the seat and sit down. Close my eyes. Remember those times riding with Pap. The excitement as he revved the engine. The thrill of rapid acceleration. Clutching to him. The laughter and the screams. The love. I open my eyes. I know renting a beat-up truck would be more practical. And of course, Pap died riding a motorcycle. But I must have this bike. It's the feeling, the nostalgia—the connection it gives me.

Across the street a gang of guys is harassing another guy. They're yelling—arguing with the guy and pushing him. One of the guys throws a cross and drops him to the ground. The rest of them pounce—kicking and stomping. The guy on the ground cries for help. I run to the entry of the lot and yell, "Hey! Stop!" But they keep going. I move into the street. "Hey! Hey! Stop it! Stop!" The group turns, points and hollers, and then starts running at me.

I burst in the garage office. "Quick! Help!" I call and point to the guys storming towards us. The owner reaches into his desk and grabs a handgun and rushes out. The guys keep charging forward. The owner raises the gun. They halt. A loud exchange ensues. The men back down and retreat out of the lot. The injured man is left alone. He climbs to his feet and limps away.

"What was that all about?" I ask Vusi.

"Skebengas—gangsters," he says.

"I was just trying to help that guy. They were beating the crap out of him."

"They don't like White men telling them what to do," the owner interjects.

"Shame. Do not take it personally," Vusi says.

I don't know how to respond, so I say nothing.

"Let's make a plan about a hiring you a car," Vusi says to change the subject.

I turn to the owner. "I'd like that motorcycle over there." And after some negotiations in Zulu, Vusi works out a deal for me to rent the bike. I actually try to buy it, but Vusi convinces me that without proper vehicle registration and the other necessary paperwork I'd get in trouble with the cops. And that's the last thing I want, so we reach an agreement to rent the bike for as long as I need or for as long as it lasts—whichever comes first. Basically, I'm buying it and paying this guy to use his paper work. He charges me twenty-thousand-rand cash. That's one-third of my current stash, but like I said, I want this bike.

I dump my clothes in the parking lot. I pack what I can into the bike's side storage pods and leave the rest on pavement. Then I roll up my stash of cash in Pap's duffel and stuff it in the back pod—along with one Bible and a set of rosary beads just in case I need to pass as a priest. The rest of the Bibles and beads I leave with Vusi. "Can you find a good home for these? Bring them to a church or something for me?"

"Shap shap. I will take care of it," he says.

"Thanks. And thanks for taking care of me. You've been a big help."

"Yebo, Victor. It is my pleasure."

"You're one of the good ones, Vusi. This world needs more people like you."

"Yoh! Thank you, my brother."

I pay Vusi for his troubles then review Mum Mary's directions with him and take his number in case I get lost. Then I give him a hug, slap on a helmet, and start up the bike. I'm shaky at first—wobbling and jerking my way through the gears. Getting a feel for the brakes and acceleration. Steadying my nerves as I motor through traffic. I had a dirt bike when I was seventeen, but I haven't ridden since then. Yet despite the danger and apprehension, it feels right to ride.

On the outskirts of Johannesburg, I ride alongside a speeding train. Teenagers cling to the side and stand on top. No harnesses. No restraints. They are surfing—freight hopping—doing twists and turns on the outside of the speeding boxcars. I pump my fist at them. And they wave. I understand them. Their flirtation with death. We are kindred spirits. Sharing the thrill of freedom—the feeling of nothing left to lose.

∞

four

There is an accident on the highway. Emergency vehicles siren and flash. Smoke rises in the distance. I weave through halted traffic until I reach the crash site. A poultry truck has flipped and caught fire. The driver is dead—lying on the pavement. Surviving chickens skitter around frantically. The rest are a mess of smoldering carcasses and blood. Burning feathers plume among the smoke. A dozen passenger cars have smashed and bottle-necked behind the truck. Injured victims sit on the side of the road—dazed. One woman screams—the white of her fractured bone piercing out of her flesh. Emergency workers rush to her aid. I idle there—and then I see him—Boris. His large bulk strewn across the road. It takes me a second to process that it's him because his skin is ground and charred—bleeding crevices filled with dirt and asphalt and blood. But I know it's him—the bald head, the leather jacket, the crushed compact car nearby. One of the chickens that miraculously survived the crash is pecking at the blood dripping down his cracked skull. I jump off my bike and run to him.

"Boris, are you okay?" Of course he isn't okay.

He gurgles some incoherent sounds. His eyes whirling in his head like a puppet.

"Boris…it's me…it's Victor!"

He gasps—and for a moment there is clarity in his eyes.

"Boris! You're going to be oaky. You were in a crash…"

"Boychick…the ferocity…" Boris starts to laugh—choking up blood. And then he gasps again—wheezing deeply—and then he passes out. I call for help—grabbing onto a passing emergency worker. They kneel next to him—checking his vitals and calling for more help. And

134

for the second time in two days, I find myself praying. I don't know what prayer looks like and sounds like for others—but this is a conflicted prayer—one of contrition and gratitude. I don't pray for Boris to live, but I don't pray for him to die either. I simply repeat, 'I'm sorry and thank you' over-and-over as I feel the anguish of this miracle swell within my chest. I pray to Pap in the great beyond—knowing he met a similar fate—and feeling for a moment, that despite being enemies, Boris and I are one and the same. The chances are finite—and yet here I kneel and here he lays—dying at my feet. My chance at freedom enhanced by his demise. Or perhaps it just means greater misery to come. But for now, I hold his hand and watch his last breaths. He dies—and I ride on—a horrific miracle receding in my rearview mirrors—hope granted in a tragic form.

∞

five

The sky is cloudy and gray. Everything feels slower—half-speed compared to my last moments in New York. Spits of rain slap against my visor. Flat brush and open plains stretch to the horizon. I ride east into hills of timbering pine and then down into a verdant valley. I stop for gas and lunch—a couple beers and a meat pie. Buy some candy and South African jerky—'biltong' it's called. Then get back on the road. I cruise along the outskirts of Nelspruit—past stadium construction for the World Cup. The sun breaks through the clouds. It's late afternoon now. The road winds along the edge of a canyon then drops down and cuts through a long stretch of lush sugar cane fields. Green mountains loom in the distance. The world is aglow in golden light. I enter the villages of the Nkomazi. Small densely packed cinderblock houses with tin roofs hug the road. Wash lines with vibrant clothes run between them. Electrical wires snake around poles. Smoke from cooking fires and burning trash rises. Pedestrians meander along the shoulders. A herd of cattle saunters into the road. I stop. A barefoot boy in torn pants prods the reluctant cows with a stick and nudges them across the tar. I pass the Matsamo Shopping Plaza—a key landmark in Mum Mary's directions—it's a crowded rundown strip mall with a grocery store, liquor store, gas station, and Kentucky Fried Chicken. On the other side of the plaza there is a faded billboard for a coffee plantation. Beside it is a small shack where an old lady is selling vegetables. I turn down the road and nod to the woman. She smiles back with a toothless grin. Red dirt kicks under my tires in a fiery cloud. Past a cluster of one-room houses and then it's open road and scrub brush.

I arrive at the old coffee plantation—Mum Mary's compound. A rusted iron fence with large coils of barbed wire surrounding it. Through the gate there is a water tower, a pair of cinderblock bunkhouses, and a wooden cabin. Further back, the main house stands surrounded by a grove of trees—a large one-level stucco home with stone columns and a covered porch. I get off my bike to open the gate. A dog rushes at me. It barks and snarls. It's big and ugly and pregnant—it's mangy skin and sagging nipples scrape the ground.

"Hello! Hello?" I call into the yard. The dog snaps at me through the gate. The latch is unlocked, but I'm not opening it with this dog trying to devour me. I keep yelling, "hello, hello" into the yard. Then I remember I have Mum Mary's number. But when I call, she doesn't answer. So I grab the bag of biltong I bought at the gas station and throw some through the fence. The dog quiets down and gobbles it up. I throw her more. Then get brave and hold out my hand with meat in my palm. She comes close, sniffs my hand, but won't eat. So I drop it and she chews. Her tail is wagging and she's stopped barking. So I try again to open the gate. But as soon as I crack it open, the dog lunges at me. I drop to the ground and cover my face—squeezing my eyes shut and waiting to be mauled. But the bite doesn't come. And when I look up, I see the dog running down the road. I take off after her. I can't let my first impression to Mum Mary be me letting her pregnant dog loose. Images of the dog getting struck by a car flash into my mind. She and her pups splattered across the pavement. So I run—huffing and puffing—all the way back to the tar road. Why I didn't just hop back on my bike, I have no idea. Regardless, I arrive back at the old woman's vegetable shack and find the dog sitting beside a kneeling boy. He's patting her and she's licking his face.

The boy looks up as I approach. "Are you the man coming to stay with us?" he asks.

"Do you live with Mum Mary?"

"Yebo, yes."

"Well then, yes—I'm the man coming to stay with you."

"You are Father Liam's brother?"

"Yup, I am. I'm Victor. What's your name?"

"My name is Themba," the boy says, "and this is Scratch," indicating the dog.

"I'm sorry—I let Scratch escape from the yard."

"No problem," he says, "she gets out all the time. Too much. That is why she is always pregnant—that is what Mum Mary says. Scratch has had many, many babies. Too many babies."

"Yeah, I can see that," I say laughing and pointing at her dragging nipples.

"You laugh like Father Liam," he says. "You look like him too."

"We're twins."

"Yebo, I know twins. Mercy, Grace, and Hope—they are also twins."

"There are three of them?"

"Yebo," he says nodding.

"Well then—they are called triplets."

"Yebo! Triplets."

"How old are you Themba?"

"Ten. How old are you?"

"Ah...wow, I have to think about that for a second—I'm thirty-three."

"One day I will be thirty-three too," he says.

"That you will. But I'll never get to be ten again like you. So enjoy it."

"Father Liam is my good friend," he says, "I think we will be good friends too."

"I hope so," I say.

"Buya, come," Themba says as he takes my hand and leads Scratch and me back up the red dirt road. We wave at the old woman,

138

and she gives us both her toothless smile. The warmth of his small hand in mine is comforting. He is a scrawny kid—I can see his ribs under his sleeveless navy t-shirt and his bony ankles below his rolled up black sweats. He's got a too big for his body sized-head and giant ears that stick out. Dark murky eyes. A bright smile.

"Victor, do you like to play marbles?" Themba asks.

"I've never played marbles."

"I will teach you. I love marbles. And drawing. And mangoes."

"I like those other things too."

"We have mango trees at Mum Mary's house. They are too good."

"What don't you like?"

"I do not like Maths. Or doing my chores. Or when Mum Mary is strict."

"Is Mum Mary mean to you?"

"No. I love Mum Mary. Too much. But she is strict. Too strict."

"How long have you lived with her? Mum Mary, I mean."

"Forever. Since I was a baby. My mother—she left me here."

"I'm sorry," I say and exhale deeply.

"That is okay. I like living with Mum Mary. But not when she makes me do the dishes. I hate to do the dishes. And I wish she would let me keep one of Scratch's puppies. I want a dog. A dog all my own. So we can play together. I would teach him to play marbles with me. But Mum Mary says she is going to cull the puppies. That makes me sad," Themba says and drops down on one knee and slings his arms around Scratch and hugs her. She licks his ear in return.

"Scratch really likes you. I thought she was going to bite me. When I went to open the gate, she lunged at me, and I fell to the ground and curled up like a baby. Just like this," I say and make a silly show of dropping to the ground, curling into a ball, and reenacting my cowardice.

Themba laughs. A wild joyous laugh. And I recognize it immediately. It's Pap—Pap's laugh. The same infectious cackle. The same jubilation. The same delight. It's uncanny. As if he were reborn here. And I can't help myself but laugh too. Which only makes Themba laugh harder. We collapse on our backs and roll around in the dirt—coughing and gasping for air in cathartic glee. Pap echoing in Themba's laughter—floating among the dust in the dying light—fading as we exhale.

The sun starts to set. The sky turns a deep purple. The wildlife of night awakens. Crickets and frogs chirp and croak through the humid air. We approach Mum Mary's gate. Themba takes my hand once more. "Why have you come here?" he asks. I surprise myself by telling him the truth. "I got in trouble," I say, "I had nowhere to go. Liam helped me escape. And Mum Mary has agreed to let me stay here."

"You are an orphan like me!"

"Yeah…yeah, I guess, I am."

"Is that your motorbike?" Themba says running towards it.

"Yes, it is."

"Can I have a ride?"

"Sure! Open the gate and hop on," I say as I slide onto the bike and start it up. Themba jumps on the back and Scratch sprints into the yard. I rev the engine and accelerate. Themba screams with laughter. I speed up to the main house and skid to a stop—trying to give Themba an extra thrill. But he isn't holding on tight enough and falls off the bike.

"Oh no!" I kill the engine and rush to him.

"That was lekker!" he cheers.

"But you're okay?"

"Yebo, yes!"

A small crowd has gathered—an older woman, two teenagers, and three young girls.

"Mr. Carroll, I presume," the woman says.

"Mum Mary?"

"Yes, yes. Welcome. However, please refrain from entering the property with such commotion. Such noise will not be tolerated. We maintain peace and tranquility here. This is a place of God."

"I'm so sorry," I say. Mum Mary is short and plump with wrinkled skin, thick glasses, and stern black opal eyes. She wears a traditional white habit and veil—along with a red roped wooden crucifix around her neck. "And…and…and I just want to say thanks," I say stuttering and continuing on, "Thanks for helping me. Thanks for saving me. For letting me come here. For helping me back at the airport. Thanks for…everything."

"Jesus is the only one who can save you. And I assume you mean to say, 'Thank you.' We do not use slang here. Only proper language. Always. It is the Lord's way. You simply must."

"Yeah, yeah, of course. I only meant that…"

"You mean 'yes, yes,' not 'yeah, yeah,'" she says cutting me off. "Slang is laziness. And laziness is the work of the devil. And we do not tolerate the devil. Right, children?" She turns to the kids standing around her.

"Yes, Mum Mary," they all say in a uniform drone.

"Do you understand?" she says turning back to me.

"Yes, Mum Mary," I say with the same drone. Mum Mary is tough. I can see now how she could have escaped Soweto, how she could have been a revolutionary smuggler during Apartheid, how she could have the stamina and heart to run a rural orphanage.

"I will get word to your brother that you have arrived safely. We have decided it is best that you do not communicate with him here. However, I will arrange for you to speak with him using an intermediary. You will accompany us to church on Sunday and we will arrange a call using Father Chimo's phone."

"Thank…ah…thank you. But I think I should talk to him immediately. That trouble at the airport. Well, it tried to follow me here. I mean…he tried to follow me here. But there was an accident. And…well…I think everything is okay for now. But maybe it's not. And…"

"I thought I informed you over the phone that I will not tolerate any troubles."

"Yeah…yes, you said that. But…I just think I need to speak with Liam."

"As I said, I will send word through the proper channels. And we will arrange a call."

"But…."

"This matter is over," she says—looking at me with the wrath of final judgment.

"Okay…Sunday it is then. But please tell Liam that I'm okay."

"Now, let me introduce you to everyone," Mum Mary says and turns to the children. The oldest, Jabulani, is eighteen—so not really a child at all—he's a driver for Mum Mary's community center and training to be a mechanic. Then there is Sabelo—sixteen. He's still in high school and wants to study computers. Next is Themba. And then, beside him, are three identical triplet girls—Mercy, Grace, and Hope—seven years old. I nod and smile at them all.

"That will be your dwelling," Mum Mary says pointing to the cabin back near the entrance to the compound. "Your brother stays there on his visits, so I trust you will find it suitable. I will have Themba bring you some linens. You missed dinner, which is always promptly at six, so you will be on your own for supper this evening. Additionally, your brother informed me that you have experience as a writer, so I have you scheduled to begin teaching English at our community center starting on Monday morning. I keep a busy schedule, so if there are any questions, please ask either Jabulani or Sabelo. They will assist you. I trust you are quite capable of taking care of yourself. So again, welcome, and please remember that this is a place of God. Good evening and God bless. That is all." And with that she turns and marches back into the house. The other children disperse as well. Except for Themba who stands beside me.

"Wow. She is a serious woman," I say.

"I told you. She is very strict. Too strict," Themba says.

"You weren't kidding."

The cabin is barebones—a wooden structure with a pitched roof and a small porch. The inside is dingy. Dust everywhere. Warped floors. Moth eaten curtains. Screenless windows. Cobweb infested corners. A rudimentary wooden desk and dresser. A moldy foam mattress. A grease laden kitchenette. A giant wooden crucifix nailed to wall. And a Virgin Mary statue lamp on the decrepit side table.

I unload the storage pods—sticking my cash in the dresser—and Themba returns with the linens. Scratch runs around him yipping at his heels. "Victor, will you teach me to drive your motorbike?"

"Of course. We can start our lessons tomorrow."

"Serious, serious?" he asks.

"Of course not," I laugh, "Mum Mary would kill me."

"Aww shame, Victor."

"Sorry, little buddy."

"Will you teach me when I am old enough?"

"If I'm still here when you are old enough to drive this thing, you can have it."

"Serious, serious?" he asks.

"It's all yours."

Themba helps me make the bed. And then while I sort through Liam's clothes, he hops back on the bike and pretends to ride—making loud racing sounds and narrating as he accelerates and jumps over imaginary cars and canyons. The three triplet girls come running toward us like fairies flying through the evening air. They shout and laugh, and when they pass, Themba jumps off the bike, and he and Scratch go chasing after them. I'm left alone standing in the bruised darkness. The faint outline of mountains in the distance. Scattered trees. Rustling wild grass. And red earth. Here I am.

Themba returns with his head hung. He is sniffling—crying.

"What's wrong?" I ask.

"Mercy, Grace, and Hope—they took my toothbrush. And they dropped it. And Scratch got it. And she ate it. And now it is broken." He holds up the remains of the brush—the top has been chewed off.

"I'm sorry. I'm really sorry," I say. "But I think I can help. Hold on." I go into the cabin and get my toiletry bag. Liam—the always prepared boy scout—packed me an extra toothbrush. "Here," I say returning outside, "now there's nothing to be upset about." Themba takes the toothbrush and then throws his arms around me and gives me a hug. "Thank you, Victor!" My heart swells. I'm taken aback. It's only a toothbrush.

The bathhouse is a square cinderblock structure in between the cabin and boy's bunk house. Inside there are two sinks, two toilet stalls, and two shower stalls with ragged curtains drawn across them. The older boys, Jabulani and Sabelo, are at the sinks washing their faces when Themba and I enter with our toothbrushes.

"Unjani, bhuti," they both say, explaining to me that it means "greetings, brother" in SiSwati. Jabulani is tall and full. Strong—but with a round face and soft belly. Sabelo is short and wiry. He wears glasses and has a pointed noise.

"Hey guys!" I say. "And hey, is it okay to drink the water here?"

"Yebo, yes," Jabulani says, "Mum Mary has her own spring well."

"But elsewhere you must not drink the water," Sabelo adds.

"Okay, good to know, thanks," I say. And while Themba and I wait to brush our teeth at the sink, I pull back one of the curtains to take a look at the shower conditions. "Whoa!" I yell and jump back. Hanging at eye level is a giant spider with tiger stripes and a golden web. It's huge—the biggest spider I've ever seen.

"Eish, sorry bhuti, that is Bafana," Jabulani says.

"Bafana?"

"Yebo. The spider's name is Bafana."

"That's the biggest spider I've ever seen."

"He is our pet," Themba says.

"He is enormous," I say.

"That shower does not work. We let him stay there. He eats the bugs," Sabelo says.

"Bafana once ate a whole snake. Eats birds too," Themba says.

"Is he poisonous?" I ask.

"Not too much," Jabulani says, "I let him walk on me once."

"What did he do?"

"He bit me. And it hurt. And it gave me a blister for a week." And at this Themba and Sabelo both laugh at him. And again, Pap returns in the echo of Themba's laughter. And I laugh too. "Well, I'm not getting anywhere near him," I say.

"He is harmless. I promise," Sabelo says.

"Yebo, harmless," Jabulani repeats.

"Yeah! So harmless he gave you a blister for a week," I say and the boys laugh again. Then Jabulani and Sabelo say goodnight, and Themba and I stand at the sink and brush our teeth. We let the paste foam in our mouths and growl and make mad dog noises in the blemished mirror.

"Let's do this," I say, "you leave your toothbrush with me. I'll hold onto it for you. That way the girls won't steal it from you again. And we can brush our teeth together at the sink in my cabin. And that way I don't have to go anywhere near that spider."

"Okay, bhuti. What about when you have to wash and use the toilet?" he asks.

"Well, I may never shower again."

I lay on the lumpy foam mattress and stare at the cabin ceiling. The light from the Virgin Mary statue lamp casts a saintly glow across the room. The air is stale and hot. Smells like moldy bread. A lizard scurries along a cross beam. Rodents skitter beneath the floorboards. Outside, the night is alive with the calls of nocturnal creatures. I think about home. About everyone: Marco and Bobby, Jinhee and Destiny, Liam and Mom. Think about how I may have a second chance—the opportunity to actually do something with my life. Escaped. Alive—for now. Boris—dead. And Noah—I have no idea what he will do now. But he will not take Boris' death in passing. So here I am. In South Africa. Alone and afraid. I go to the desk and open its single drawer. There is a notepad there. And a pen. I can see the imprint of Liam's handwriting scratched into the page. I scribble. Then write: *Somewhere deep in the night of Africa, something breaks open inside of me. And from the cracks, a new being emerges. Crawling from the cesspool of my past. Unfettered. I awaken. I Stand. Walk. Yearn. Breathe again.* I stop there. Read back over what I wrote. And I laugh. Rip out the page. Crumple it. Toss it on the floor. I go to the dresser. Check on the money. Wink at the Virgin Mary lamp. Fall into bed. Sleep.

∞

six

"Good morning, bhuti!" Themba stands over me holding a mango. Scratch stands next to him wagging her tail. My foot is hanging off the bed and she licks it. I forgot to lock the cabin last night. "Thanks for the toothbrush," he says handing me the mango.

"It was nothing. Thanks for this," I say as I sit up in bed.

"I picked it from the tree. From the very top. I climbed all the way. The best ones are always the hardest to reach." I rise to my feet, rub my eyes, and stretch. My head is cloudy—I haven't slept so long in a while. Themba and I go outside and sit on the stoop. It's early still. Sun rising through the morning haze. I bite the mango. It's ripe and sweet. The juice runs down my face. Drips on my fingers. Themba removes a mango of his own from his pocket and takes a bite. Scratch lays at our feet. With his free hand, Themba massages her swollen belly.

"When are her puppies coming?" I ask.

"Two weeks," Themba says with certainty.

"This mango is amazing," I say. And no sooner do the words leave my mouth than Themba is running across the yard and jumping up into the mango tree—Scratch jiggling close behind him. He climbs with ease, picks four from the top, sacks them in his shirt, shimmies down the tree one handed, and returns to the stoop and dumps them at my feet.

"Wow. You are fast," I say as we both pick up mangoes and take bites.

"Too fast!" he says.

We brush our teeth at the kitchenette sink in the cabin—making mad dog sounds again.

"I hope this becomes our routine. Eating mangoes and brushing our teeth together," I say.

"Me too, Victor!"

I excuse myself and go to the bathhouse for a shower. For a moment, I forget about Bafana the spider and pull back the curtain on his stall. I jump back. A giant beetle is trapped in his golden web—flittering—unable to escape. The water is freezing. There is no hot water tank. But that's no matter as a quick rinse is fine on account of Bafana in the stall beside me.

I step back out onto the cabin porch after getting dressed. Liam packed me nothing but khaki shorts and dorky polo shirts. Hopefully, I'll lose a little weight here, and at least fit into them. Mum Mary comes marching towards me from the main house. As she approaches, Jabulani, Sabelo, and Themba come outside of their bunk house as well.

"Good Morning, boys," she says.

"Good Morning, Mum Mary," they say in the same uniform rote as last night.

"Good morning, Victor," she says.

"Good morning, Mum Mary," I say back in the same rote manner.

"Listen up," she says to turning to the boys, "today, I will be driving to Nelspruit to meet with a potential funder. I will be back later this evening. Victor, as it is Saturday and the center is closed, you will accompany and assist Jabulani and Sabelo on their weekend deliveries of medication and food parcels to patients and caregivers. Pay close attention, as this will be one of the weekly duties I expect you to perform while you are here. But first, you will take Themba and the girls to Mum Siphiwe's house. Understood?"

"Yea, of course. I mean…yes, of course. Glad to help."

"Very well," she says.

"Mum Mary, may I please go with Victor and the other boys on their duties today?" Themba asks. "Please? I promise to behave. And I will do extra chores in the garden. And wash the dishes every night."

"It's fine by me," I say in support.

"Excuse me," she says turning to me, "it does not matter what is 'fine' and 'not fine' by you—as you say. These children are my wards. They are my responsibility. Not yours."

"Oh. I didn't mean any disrespect. I was just trying to…"

"What you were 'trying to do' has no impact on the matter."

"Yes, Mum Mary," I say hanging my head like a scolded child.

"As for you," she says turning back to Themba, "you know you are not permitted to speak out of turn. For that, you will most certainly be performing extra chores in the garden. As well as doing the dishes every night next week. However, I am inclined to allow you to accompany the others on their duties. You are old enough now. You must learn as well."

"I am sorry, Mum Mary. Thank you, Mum Mary," Themba responds dutifully—trying to suppress a smile. Then as she turns her back to give Jabulani and Sabelo further instructions, he slips me a big thumbs-up. And I give him two back.

"Well that was something," I say when Mum Mary is out of earshot.

"You will get used to it," Sabelo says.

"Yes. She cares for us very much. But eish! She is too strict," Jabulani says.

"Yebo. Too, too strict," Sabelo echoes.

"Four strict!" Themba yells. It takes a second for his joke to land. But then we all laugh.

We leave Mum Mary's compound in an old pick-up truck. Or a 'bakkie' as Themba explains it's called in South Africa. Jabulani drives. Sabelo rides in the cab beside him. Me and Themba and the triplets sit in the back on the open flat bed. It's hot and humid—the sun beating down on us—radiating off the metal. The truck is filled with supplies—sacks of corn meal, jugs of water, bottles of oil, crates of eggs, bags of onions, tomatoes, and cabbage, parcels of medicine, and stacks of newspapers.

We stop first at the plaza to drop off the newspapers. Mum Mary's center publishes it—*The Nkomazi Times*. As I help the boys haul the stacks off the truck, I glance at the headline: "Knockout Curse! Sangoma Dies During Epic Battle with Tokoloshe."

"What is a Tokoloshe?" I ask. The boys laugh and talk back-and-forth in SiSwati. Sabelo takes off his glasses and cleans them with his shirt. "A Tokoloshe is a bad demon that curses people and causes them much harm," he says.

"And you believe in them?"

"Yebo!" he says as he puts his clean glasses back on his face.

"Come on! Are you serious? They can't be real."

"Not real for you. But for us, they are real," Jabulani says.

"What do you mean?"

"You do not believe, so they cannot hurt you. We believe so, they can hurt us," he says.

"That makes no sense."

"It is not your culture. But in our culture, we believe," Sabelo says.

I turn to Themba. "Are they joking with me? You really believe in these things?"

"Yebo, yes," he says. "Sho! They are very bad. Serious, serious."

We drop off the triplets with Mum Siphiwe. She is one of the caregivers who works for Mum Mary. Her house is a crumbling cinderblock structure with a tin roof. A clothes line, a big plastic water tank, an outhouse, and a small corn field surround it. Mum Siphiwe comes out from behind her hanging laundry as we pull-up. Five kids around the triplets' age run out behind her. Mum Siphiwe is old and frail. But her grip is strong. She puts her rough hands on my cheeks and looks into my eyes—a powerful stare. "You are my new American son," she says, "Father Liam is my other American son. I will be your mother while you are here in South Africa."

"I'm honored," I say. "Are these your other children?" indicating the kids beside her.

"I am much too old to have children," she laughs. Mum Siphiwe explains how Mum Mary runs her orphanage. The Nkomazi region has a forty percent HIV positive rate. As such, there are a tragic number of orphans—far too many for one central orphanage. So Mum Mary came up with the ingenious plan of paying the older women in the community—the grandmothers or 'gogos' in SiSwati—to take care of the orphans. Many orphans are also HIV positive, which is why in addition to unloading a food parcel for Mum Siphiwe and the children, we also drop off antiretroviral medications as well.

We spend the morning dropping off rations and medications to other caretakers. The experience is an uncanny mixture of tragedy and the sublime. Delivering the necessities of survival to sick kids without parents. Riding in the open air through idyllic pastures. Feeding hungry children in tattered clothes. Themba leaning against me and singing "Three Little Birds" as we rumble across red dirt roads.

"How do you know Bob Marley?" I yell.

"How do you know Bob Marley?" he echoes back.

"Everyone knows Bob Marley," I yell.

"Yebo, yes! Everyone knows Bob Marley!" And I join him in singing.

At the last stop of the morning, Jabulani and Sabelo stay in the truck to rest. "It is too hot," they say. So Themba and I unload the rations. While we do, a leftover newspaper falls from the flatbed. I pick it up, and again see the headline about demon possession. Handing the paper back into the truck to Themba, I ask, "Do you really believe in demons?"

"I know you do not believe, Victor. But I believe."

"Have you ever seen one?"

"No. But I feel them. I have demons living inside me."

"What do you mean?"

"Ask Mum Mary, she will tell you. I have demons—like the Tokoloshe."

"Okay, but what do you really mean by that?"

"I take those medicines," he says pointing to the bag of antiretrovirals in my hand.

"Wait. I'm confused. You mean, you have HIV?"

"Yebo, yes. HIV. The virus. It is a demon that lives inside of me."

My chest rips open. I grab Themba and hug him. He startles but then hugs me back. I want to fix him. Make him better. Promise him that everything will be okay—that he will be okay. And to have the power to deliver on that promise. "I'm sorry" is all I can muster.

"Do not worry, Victor," he says, "I am happy. So you must be happy too. Mum Mary says everyone has demons inside them. But that some demons are worse than other demons. So you have demons too. Just like me. But do not be worried. You will be okay. I will be okay too. So you must be happy. Just like Bob Marley says."

"Mum Mary and Bob Marley are wise. And you're a pretty smart kid too," I say.

We carry the supplies into the dirt yard of another cinderblock home. A group of excited kids comes running towards us. A gogo hobbles after them. Themba walks tall—proud to be of service. A heaping pile of salty french fries stands before us. I'm paying. So the boys ordered extra. We've stopped for lunch at a roadside stall made of fence posts and corrugated tin. Themba demonstrates the proper way to eat these 'slap chips' by lathering them in vinegar and wrapping them in spongy white bread. They're delicious. And remind me of 'Triple Whites.' As we eat, I relish not only the flavor of the salt and fat and yeast trickling across my palate, but also the nostalgic memories of me and Liam. I am eager to talk to him tomorrow. To thank him. To see if he is okay. To find out what trouble still lurks.

∞

seven

A toddler squats in the dirt fiddling with a toy car made from elastics and wire hangers. He is naked and malnourished—dirt and dried snot stick to his upper lip. He smiles when he sees us. And Themba goes to him. Brings him water. Gives him a mango. Sits down beside him. Fixes the band that holds the wheels. Starts playing with him.

We enter a dilapidated structure. A dying woman lays across a bare mattress on the cement floor. An ancient gogo sits in a folding chair beside her—praying. We greet them. All afternoon we've been delivering medications and pain killers to palliative care patients. People starved of food and opportunity. Drowning in suffering and injustice. Stricken with AIDS. But not without dignity. Mum Mary has assured this—by providing pills to relieve their pain and companionship to soothe their loneliness—by paying the gogos to hold vigil with the sick so that no one dies alone.

This woman is disintegrating. Emaciated Bones. Pustulating lesions. Flies buzzing. The smell of sick. She groans—about to die. Jabulani and Sabelo kneel beside her. Give her a pain pill and some water. She chokes. But gets it down. They ease her back. Her breath is shallow. She wheezes. Moans. Struggles. Gasps. Dies.

The gogo prays over the woman's body in silent mourning. I help Jabulani and Sabelo wrap her in a blanket and carry her to the truck. Themba is still playing outside with the toddler. I bend down and join them as Jabulani and Sabelo reenter the woman's shack.

"Is she dead?" Themba asks.

"Yeah, I'm afraid so," I say.

"The dead woman is his mother."

"I figured as much."

"His father is dead too."

"What will happen to him?"

"We will take him to Mum Mary."

"What's his name?"

Themba turns and whispers to the boy—remnants of mango stick to their fingers. "His name is Lazarus. And he wants to be a race car driver when he grows older," he says pushing the boy's toy car through the dirt and kicking up a plume of dust. Jabulani and Sabelo reemerge from the woman's shack assisting the gogo. We all load into the truck.

A gust of wind blows the blanket off the dead woman's face. Luckily, Themba keeps Lazarus distracted by playing a version of Rock, Paper, Scissors called 'Ching-Chong-Cha.' I grab the blanket and hold it covered. It's agonizing—watching Lazarus ride alongside the body of his dead mother. Perhaps he is too young to fully comprehend that she is dead. Still, the morbid solemnity of this moment will remain with him—murky glimpses of this tragic memory rippling through his consciousness forever.

We drop the body with the local undertaker—a simple concrete garage with rudimentary wooden coffins lining the wall—then pick up the triplets from Mum Siphiwe. I don't understand what Themba says to them in SiSwati, but as they load into the back of the truck, they all hug and tickle Lazarus at the same time—enveloping him with love. He giggles and smiles.

Back at the compound, Mum Mary stands over Lazarus as Jabulani and Sabelo relay the news of his mother's death. She bends toward him, puts both her hands on his shoulders, and stares into his eyes. "Your mother is dead. You are alone now. Your life has been difficult. The rest of your life will be difficult too. You must accept Jesus.

Have faith. God will provide. He will take care of you. I will take care of you. Do you understand?"

Lazarus nods—tears welling in his eyes.

"Crying will not help," Mum Mary says. "Crying will not bring back your mother. Only God will provide. Have faith in Jesus. Your name is Lazarus. A blessed name. And like your namesake, you will rise again. With us. With Jesus. Now—do you understand?" Lazarus nods again—sniffling up his tears. "Very well. Come along." She takes him by the hand and leads him to the main house—to his new life.

eight

Late afternoon—the day sticks to me even after a cold shower. I ride down to the plaza and buy a bottle of whiskey. Lay on my bed—sweating—washing away painful images with every sip of amber liquid. Thoughts of Lazarus's mother laying there. Gasping for breath—for life. Her last exhale like the hiss of a snake—death announcing its arrival. Lazarus sitting outside in the dirt. Themba—so sweet—sitting beside him. Themba who will die like Lazarus' mother someday. Consumed by the virus—by the cruel world. I think of Marco too. His body mangled on the pavement. I miss him—love him—even if he's the reason for this whole mess.

"Victor! Buya! Come quick!" Themba yells as he runs into the cabin.

"What is it? Is everything alright?"

"Jabulani and Sabelo told me to fetch you. They need your help."

I go outside confused—tipsy. Jabulani and Sabelo are loading audio equipment into a BMW—a black rusted 333i model from the 80s. It's got scratches and dents all over it. As I approach, I see cracked leather and stuffing coming out of the seats inside. "Is that your car?" I ask.

"Yebo!" Jabulani says, "we bought it with our own money."

"Jabulani and Sabelo are DJs!" Themba calls out.

"So that's what all this equipment is about then," I say.

"Yes—we are working tonight," Sabelo says.

"And we are taking you out with us," Jabulani says.

"For some real Nkomazi culture," Sabelo adds.

"Sho! For some real Nkomazi culture!" Jabulani shouts.

"Thanks guys. But I'd prefer to just relax and drink," I say holding up the whiskey.

"Victor! Shame!" Jabulani says.

"You must come with us," Sabelo says.

"You simply must," Jabulani says imitating Mum Mary.

"You simply must!" Themba repeats and laughs his wild laugh.

"Fine, fine—twist my arm," I say.

"Shap, shap!" Sabelo exclaims.

"But you must first help us push-start," Jabulani instructs.

"What?" I say.

"The clutch. It is bad. We must push-start the car to make it go," Sabelo explains.

"Seriously?" I ask.

"Yebo, yes!" Themba says. "It is too much fun, Victor. Too much fun!"

"Now I know why you guys invited me—free labor," I say with a grin. Then toss my whiskey bottle into the car and help load the rest of the equipment. The trunk is so full with wires and speakers that we have to use a bungee cord to fasten it shut.

"Three, two, one…go!" we start pushing on Jabulani's command. Me and him up front. Sabelo and Themba at the back. Groaning and grunting—the car lurches forward. We huff-and-puff and get it rolling—moving faster-and-faster, pushing harder-and-harder—Jabulani jumps into the driver's seat and pops the clutch. The engine starts and revs and the car takes off. Sabelo hops in the back. But I stop—amazed this actually worked.

"Buya! Run!" Jabulani and Sabelo yell back to me.

Themba pushes me. "Go, Victor! Go!" So I run—sprint—and jump into the passenger seat. Themba cheers and I wave back at him. At Scratch too—who barks and wags her tail at us. I crack open the whiskey and take a swig—choke on it as I catch my breath—a fiery burst shoots through my lungs. Jabulani and Sabelo laugh. I pass the bottle over to

Jabulani. He rattles something to Sabelo in SiSwati, then takes the bottle and drinks. "Please bhuti," he says, "you must not tell Mum Mary about this. She forbids us to drink."

"My lips are sealed," I say.

"Do you smoke dagga?" Sabelo asks.

"Dagga? What's that? Like weed?"

"This," Sabelo says as he extends a freshly rolled joint into the front seat.

"Oh, yeah," I say with a laugh, "I smoke dagga."

Sabelo lights the joint and passes it to me.

"I'm going to assume I shouldn't tell Mum Mary about this either." I say.

We drive off the tar road and into the cane fields. The car shakes as we rumble over the uneven terrain. Branches whip through the open windows. A steady line of cars and trucks extend in front and behind us. We enter a clearing—a makeshift parking lot—where stereos are blaring and people are drinking and dancing. We drive passed them and arrive at the entry gate to a haphazard stadium constructed of piecemeal lumber and steel.

A crowd blocks the gate. Cheers and moans and cries erupt. A toothless old drunk and his mangy emaciated donkey impede the line of cars from passing. Suddenly, a dazzling Range Rover comes speeding up the road—overtaking the line of traffic—and skidding to a halt in front of the stadium entrance. A group of South African Boris-like thugs exit the SUV—the driver coming around to open the passenger door. A big fat man in a fancy suit exits and saunters to the old drunk. The old man screams and curses at the fat man. Then picks up a stone and throws it at him. The fat man's thugs pull out guns and take aim—but the fat man waves them back. He dusts off his suit. Then calmly picks the fist-size rock up from the earth and without hesitation smashes it across the old man's face. I jump back in terror. And gasp as the surrounding crowd cheers. The old man tries to stagger to his knees—his jaw shattered and bleeding. The fat man strikes the old man with the rock again. Then again. And again. The crowd erupts with applause. And the old man's donkey bleats in agony—somehow sensing the atrocity. But the crowd has it out for this mangy beast now too—adding to this delirium of violence by picking up rocks and stoning the donkey to death. The old man and his beast lay dead in a shattered heap—the corpses dragged off into a ditch. The fat man and his thugs return to the Range Rover and the flow of traffic resumes into the stadium.

"What was that?" I say in shock, "They just executed that guy."

Sabelo takes off his glasses to clean them. "That man," he says, "that fat man. He is Nkosi. King Nkosi. He owns all the Nkomazi. This whole area. He owns all the taxis. He owns all the girls. He owns all the drugs. He owns much of the land too. This land here. This is his land. He hires it to the sugar company. And he lets us use it for spinning and parties. His brother is the MP of Mpumalanga—C.C. Nkosi. Together they are very powerful. Very corrupt. They control everything."

"And he can just get away with killing people?"

"Here—he can do anything he wants," Jabulani says.

"What will happen to the body? And the donkey?" I ask.

"Vultures." They say in unison.

∞

nine

Smoke and the smell of burning rubber. Cars spin around-and-around the makeshift stadium. It's a vehicle rodeo with drivers turning their cars while hanging out the windows and doing tricks until their tires burst. Awards based on the length of the spin and the style of the driver. Spectators crowd the surrounding platforms and cheer. And when it's all over, the cars are cleared, the stands are emptied, and the masses pour down into the arena. A massive party ensues with pulsing beats, strobing lights, and grinding bodies. Jabulani and Sabelo are the DJ and MC presiding over all of it.

The world goes wavy. The three of us have finished the whiskey. I stand behind Jabulani and Sabelo surveying the scene. I spot a woman in the crowd. I am drawn to her through a silent vortex. The rest of the night vanishes around her. And I can see only her. She is beautiful. Radiant. Her body glows in a yellow dress and banded golden jewelry. She has a long neck, round eyes, and cropped hair. She moves effortlessly in rhythm with the music—in harmony with the universe. A strong and supple spirit flowing in synchronicity. I am entranced. And she catches me staring. So I dart my eyes away. But when I look back, she is smiling—waving for me to come near.

I jump off the platform into the gyrating masses. We find each other amidst the throng.

"Hello," I mouth silently under the booming music.

"Unjani," she yells over the roar. Then takes my hand and leads me away. We float through the crowd and up onto a grassy hill overlooking the stadium. A scattering of people sit around drinking and smoking. Tall stadium lights rise up and shine down upon the party. A

161

generator hums in the night air. The cane fields beyond the stadium seem infinite in the extending darkness.

"What is your name?" she asks.

"Victor. What's yours?"

"Ayanda."

"Ayanda. That's a beautiful name."

"Sit," she says crossing her legs gracefully in the grass.

"Ah. Alright," I say and flop down beside her awkwardly. I stare. At a loss.

"What are you thinking, Victor?"

"You're beautiful. Sorry, I'm drunk. I mean, you are beautiful. But I just mean…"

"You are a funny man," Ayanda says slapping my shoulder playfully.

"Is that a good thing or a bad thing?" I ask.

"You came here with those boys?" She says pointing at Jabulani and Sabelo.

"Yeah. I'm staying with them."

"You know Mum Mary?"

"Yeah, yeah. That's who I'm staying with—Mum Mary. You know her?"

"Mum Mary has my baby," she whispers while dropping her head.

"What do you mean? She has your baby?"

"She takes care of my baby."

"At her orphanage?"

"Yebo. I had my baby when I was very young. Too young. Fourteen," Ayanda says and begins to cry. Her sobs pierce my heart. I want to kiss her. It's an inappropriate impulse. But her sadness. Her beauty. Her vulnerability. I want to kiss her. Take care of her. I want to believe that I am strong and brave and true. That my passion can

162

comfort her. But that's just fantasy—a toxic iteration of my ego. Real love deserves compassion. Ayanda deserves compassion. I don't know her. But I know her. She deserves it. So I rest my hand on her back. And listen to her cry with an open heart of silent support. Her tears drip down her face and into the grass. She leans her head against mine. And I hold my breath—trying to preserve the delicate balance of this moment—like a butterfly landing on my shoulder.

"Victor!" Sabelo calls as he comes charging up the hill.

"Hey Sabelo! I was just…" But he ignores me and starts screaming at Ayanda in SiSwati. Her response is equally combative. They gesticulate wildly—their voices growing louder and louder—until Ayanda jumps up and runs back down the hill into the crowd.

"What the hell was that about?" I ask.

"I'm sorry Victor. We should have told you not to wander off."

"But I was just talking to her."

"It is dangerous for you to be alone."

"Again—I was just talking to her?"

"That girl. She is a prostitute."

"What do you mean? How do you know? We were just talking."

"I know these things, bhuti. She is one of King Nkosi's girls. She is trouble."

"But we were just talking."

"She wants your money. She thinks you have money. She is dangerous."

"I don't think so. You don't know her."

"I know her. I know them all. These prostitutes. They are all sick. With HIV."

"Look. Even if that's true. We were just talking."

"It does not matter, bhuti. You must not talk to her."

"I still don't understand. Explain."

163

"She belongs to the fat man. The man who killed the old man and his donkey. King Nkosi. That girl. She belongs to him. You cannot speak to her. It will bring us too much trouble."

I see King Nkosi down below in the stadium leaning on his Range Rover. He is bulbous—in a flashy silver suit and purple tie. And I see Ayanda too. He calls her over to him. Pats his lap. And she sits. Kisses his cheek. He fondles her breast. She pulls away. He yanks her back. She protests. He slaps her face. Scolds her. She freezes. Then snuggles into the fat of his neck and whispers into his ear. He runs his hand under her dress and between her legs. She pushes his hand away. And he slides it back. She resigns herself. Looks off into the distance. Looks up at me. I stare back—heart wrenched.

I turn to Sabelo. "Does Mum Mary know you work with that guy?"

"Mum Mary—she is the one who got us the job."

"Mum Mary! Really? Does she know he's a criminal?"

"Yebo! She says it is better to surprise the devil than to let the devil surprise you. She got us these jobs so that we may watch him. And report back to her. Mum Mary—she is a very smart woman. Too smart."

"Too smart indeed," I say. And we lean against the light post and smoke a joint. I watch and yearn for Ayanda—for her love, for her safety. Smoke rises into the night—prayer offerings for a better tomorrow.

ten

Hungover—I'm seated in the back pew of Our Lady of Fatima Chapel in the small farming town of Malelane. The mangos Themba picked for us this morning along with the toothpaste from our brushing ritual are churning in my stomach. I've thrown up in a lot of places—but church would be a first. Up on the alter Father Chimo—tall and lean from Mozambique—delivers a homily about the dangers of xenophobia. Mum Mary sits up front in the first pew with the triplets. The girls are dressed in angelic lace gowns that compliment Mum Mary's white habit. Jabulani, Sabelo, and Themba sit in the back with me. They pull constantly at their collars and ties—a Mum Mary church requirement. The pews are filled. Open windows and a singular ceiling fan do little to cool the morning humidity hanging around us. Themba and I play tic-tac-toe in the blank pages of the hymnal until the Mass is over. Afterwards, lemonade and tea are served in the shaded courtyard of the white stucco church. This is when Father Chimo calls me into the sacristy room behind the altar and hands me the phone.

"Victor."

"Liam."

"Are you okay?"

"Yeah…is it safe to speak openly?"

"I think so…I'm calling from the Cardinal's office."

"Does he know about me and the situation?"

"Of course not! He's just doing me a favor."

"Listen…that guy I told you about…Boris!"

"He's coming after you…"

"He's dead!"

"What?"

"I saw him with my own eyes. In a car crash."

"Wow! That's a prayer answered."

"Is it a sin to say that?"

"Probably…but I'm glad you're okay."

"Do you think I'm safe?"

"I don't know—they may send more people."

"Yeah…"

"Listen…Victor! Those two cops came back again after you left."

"Are you okay?"

"Yeah…I'm fine. I think I convinced them I hate you and would never help you."

"Do you? Hate me?"

"Of course not! But they were clear…if you ever come back… you're dead."

"I assumed that already. What if Noah finds out you helped me? About your passport?"

"I assume he'll kill me."

"Liam!"

"Well…it's true. So you have to stay put."

"And you really think they'll send more guys for me?"

"Maybe…maybe not. But you can't make any mistakes."

"I know…"

"So you're there now…for as long as it takes."

"For as long as it takes," I repeat.

There is a long silence on the phone. We listen to each other breathe.

"I found that Triple White sandwich you packed me," I say.

"I thought you'd appreciate that."

"Can we talk again soon?"

"Yeah. But only through third parties—to be safe."

"Liam. I love you. And not just because you're my brother."

"I know. Same. I love you too, Victor."

∞

eleven

I pull my mattress outside and lay in the afternoon shade. A gentle breeze sways the boughs of the tree canopy above. Blue sky kaleidoscopes with green leaves. The triplets run and giggle across the yard. Jabulani and Sabelo wash their car. Scratch lays pregnant in the tall grass. Themba sits beside me. Empties a bag of marbles in the dirt. Draws a circle with his finger. Then plays—shooting and crashing and rocketing glass orbs across the earth. He's dexterous and precise—hangs his tongue out sideways and squints one eye as he takes aim. There is a simple joy in watching him—as if this moment is the only moment that has ever mattered.

"Victor! You must play marbles with me," Themba announces.

"I've never played."

"It is easy. I will teach you," he says.

"Sure. Why not," I say flipping over on my stomach and leaning off the mattress. Themba demonstrates the proper technique. I pick up the shooter and take aim. It thuds out of my hand like a wet fart—plodding forward into the dirt mere inches—the rest of the marbles untouched in mocking isolation. And Themba laughs—so hard—that immaculate infectious cackle. And I'm catapulted—out of my body and into the ether—residing for moment in bliss-filled rapture.

I confide in Themba. Call it the heat. Call it the shade. Call it the daze of the hangover and the exhaustion. Call it the collision of the marbles. Or the moldiness of the mattress. Or the sweat on my back. Call it the comfort of an unlikely friendship—the wild fading remnants of Pap that echo in Themba's glorious laughter. Call it what you will—but I confide in him. I tell him everything—my whole sordid tale—all the details up until now. Glossing over the salacious parts not fit for a ten-year old of course. But basically, I tell him everything. And he listens—his marbles spinning and ricocheting through the dirt.

"Themba...what I'm trying to tell you...I've been a bad person," I conclude.

Themba pauses from his game. He looks up at me. Smiles. "Victor, you are not a bad person. You are a good person. You are my friend. My brother. So you are not a bad person. But you are very bad at marbles," he says. And the laughter returns.

∞

twelve

I take a chance at dinner. I buy a bottle of wine at the plaza and bring it up to the main house. Mum Mary is happy to have it. "It is the only alcohol worthy of consumption. It is biblical. Jesus turned water into wine. It is one of his miracles," she says with a smile. It's the first time I've seen her display an emotion other than stern piety. I open the bottle on the patio and pour her a glass. We sit in wicker chairs under the shade of the veranda. The afternoon air blows cool against the stone bricks of the house. "We live in a small community," Mum Mary explains as she takes a sip, "And like all small communities, people indulge in gossip. I never purchase wine for myself or partake of it in public as hearsay about sinful behavior would surely grow and spread." I understand her point. The gossip about Pap after he died—and about Mom's drinking—was infuriating. So I can only imagine what the headlines in the local papers might read here: "Nutty Drunk Nun Abuses Angel Orphans!"

"Back at home, all the priests drink—a lot," I say. "Liam excluded."

"Priests drinks plentifully here as well. Father Chimo drinks enough brandy to drown all of Africa. But there is a double standard for women, especially religious women. I must be precise and judicious in my actions and appearances at all times."

"That double standard exists back home too—everywhere."

Dinner is a stew—more like a mush. Themba prepared the meal as part of his chores. Onions and frozen vegetables fried in oil served with stewed chicken and corn meal. It looks abhorrent, but actually smells pretty good. We gather around the kitchen table as Mum Mary says a blessing. Themba yells out a resounding "Amen." The triplets are served first and then the boys. And as soon as they have their food, they all run outside to eat on the patio.

Mum Mary invites me to dine with her. So I pour two more glasses of wine, grab my bowl of mush, and follow her into the central living area. It's a spacious room with high pitched ceilings and a large bamboo fan. Religious inspired tapestries hang on the walls along with a metal crucifix. Unstained wooden chairs and a rectangular dining table rest atop a brightly colored woven rug.

We eat in silence. The stew is palatable—and the wine helps. But the quiet is intolerable. So I retreat to the kitchen for the rest of the wine, and without refusal, I refill Mum Mary's glass to the brim and pour what's left into my own. I wait for the wine to soak in and inspire conversation, and then ask, "Is it true what Liam told me about your past?"

"That depends entirely on what it is he has told you," she says.

"That you were an anti-apartheid activist—that you were a freedom fighter."

"I suppose there is some truth to those statements." Mum Mary proceeds to recount the details of her past. It takes some prodding and repeated questioning, along with more sips of wine, but eventually she shares. She speaks matter-of-factly—with humility and self-deprecation—but even so, the events of her life are astounding. An orphan child—her parents murdered—she grew up in the poorest and most dangerous area of the Soweto township. Adopted and educated by nuns—she had a religious awakening after being attacked as a teenager. And thereafter studied and joined the Sisters of the Immaculate Blood. Dedicated to ministering to the sick and the poor—dedicated to fighting injustice—it was only natural for her to become a revolutionary. "When a rich man's dog lives a better life than a rich man's worker—we have a moral imperative to fight," she says. And fight she did: protesting, smuggling supplies, caring for the wounded, relaying secret communications, giving sanctuary to fellow freedom fighters—she did it all. Some of which she will not say. And then after apartheid ended, she continued her fight—moving out here to care for orphans and battle AIDS. It's like Liam said, Mum Mary is a bad ass.

"What motivates you? What keeps you going?" I ask.

"It is imperative that you understand one simple idea. A fundamental truth. Faith. Faith motivates me. Faith is responsible for goodness and joy. You must understand—God is not a table, Victor," Mum Mary says tapping out these final words on the wood and finishing her last sip of wine.

"God is not a table?"

"God is not a table."

"I don't understand."

"This table. It was constructed by men. It was created by ego. Religion is constructed by men. Created by ego. God is not religion. God is not a table. God is not ego. In Exodus when Moses asks the burning bush how it shall be defined, it answers 'I am that I am.' That is God. Infinite unity and love. Faith. All else is a divisive manifestation of the ego. Churches, rituals, laws—these are the preferences of the powerful men who created them. Men who act as gods are the cause of evil. But God is not a table. Humble faith is the only way to know God—to know truth and justice. Do you have faith, Victor?"

"I'm an atheist—so no."

"You do not need to believe in God to have faith."

"Isn't that the very definition of faith?"

"You have not been listening. God is not a man. God is not a religion. 'Ubuntu,' we say in South Africa. It is a Zulu word meaning 'universal togetherness.' God is 'ubuntu.' Infinite unity and love. God is not a table."

"Forgive me. Maybe I've had too much wine. But I just don't understand. I mean, I get the God as 'infinite love' thing. And I can certainly get behind this whole 'Ubuntu' idea. But I'm confused. You're Catholic. Doesn't that mean you adhere to a specific religion. And what about Jesus? You said 'God is not a man.' But you worship Jesus. Wasn't Jesus a man?"

"Yes, I am Catholic. But my religion is how I practice my faith, not how I define it. I am first-and-foremost a catholic—with a lower case 'c'—which means 'universal.' We are all catholic—universal citizens of humanity. All religious traditions have 'ubuntu' at their roots—they all have faith. Jesus was a prophet of love. Jesus knew God. But the temples built in his name, the wars fought in his name, the people persecuted in his name—these are acts of the ego. These are tables. God is not a table. You do not need to fully understand this now. You do not need to believe in God. You must merely have faith. And then—one day—you will understand."

My head spins with wine and lofty visions of tables and gods. Themba is waiting for me back at the cabin. He's sitting on the stoop rubbing Scratch's pregnant belly. We grab our toothbrushes and decide on the bathhouse for our brushing ritual this evening. Bafana the spider is weaving a webbed sac around an ensnared garden snake. We jitter and twitch in the mirror—imitating the snake's futile attempts at escape. And though I may not fully comprehend Mum Mary's enlightened spiritual philosophy, I understand the simplicity of brotherhood and love—the great joy of togetherness—my faith in Themba's wild laughter.

∞

thirteen

The fingers of dawn stretch out over the mountains in the distance. A morning fog pervades the landscape—hovering just above the tall grass and dancing in the wind. Themba arrives at my cabin carrying mangos and dressed in his school uniform—navy blue slacks and a light blue oxford.

"Unjani, bhuti!" he says.

"It's my first day of work today—wish me luck."

"You do not need luck. You will be great," he says handing me a mango.

"Thanks buddy."

"But Victor—first you must lift me to school on your motorbike?"

"I must?"

"Please. Please will you lift me to school on your motorbike."

"I'm not sure how Mum Mary will feel about that."

"I have already asked her. She said that it was okay," he says with a grin.

"Why do I get the feeling that you are lying?"

"Because Mum Mary will never allow me if I ask."

"Exactly...But I'm going to pretend you did ask."

"So will you give me a ride to school on your motorbike?"

"Yes—but if you get in trouble, don't blame me."

"Yoh! I promise."

"If she asks, I'm saying you told me you had permission."

"Yebo, Victor! Yebo!"

The bike starts up with a roar. I look over my shoulder expecting to see Mum Mary coming out of her house to chastise me for the noise. But her sedan is already gone. Themba opens the gate. And Scratch escapes down the road. I slap my helmet on Themba and he hops on the back looking like a toy bobble head. We take off—fast—ripping through the fog along the red dirt road.

"Go home, Scratch!" Themba yells as we pass.

"Go home!" I echo. And we laugh.

We reach the tar road and stop to wave at the toothless gogo in her vegetable shack. Then I turn back to Themba. "Hold on tight," I say. He hugs his arms around me. We blast off—racing—concrete houses and scrub brush blurring around us.

"Faster! Faster!" Themba screams. I accelerate again—dodging and weaving around cattle and traffic. The engine howls and we tear down a long straight away through the cane fields. The sky burns pink around us and the stalks glisten with dew. I close my eyes—traveling faster still. Thoughts cease. Speed and wind and Themba's arms are all I sense. This is paradise—ubuntu—Mum Mary's faith.

Caught in a speed trap. I get pulled over. For going criminally fast. By a fat local cop sitting in a lawn chair with a radar detector under the shade of a tree. His buddy idling in a squad car further down the road in the cane fields. The cop threatens to arrest me. I try to tell him that I'm a priest. That I'm Liam—a holy man here for missionary work. But he doesn't care. I tell him that if he lets me go, I will pray for him and give him blessings. I even take the remaining Bible and rosary beads from the rear storage pod and offer them to him—promise him salvation in the afterlife. But again, he doesn't care. Although, he does says he'll let me go if I buy him a cold drink. "I'm thirsty," he says.

"I'm sorry, but I don't have any drinks," I say.

"He wants money," Themba whispers to me.

"You mean bribe him?"

"Yebo. He is thirsty for money. I have seen this with Mum Mary."

"You've seen Mum Mary bribe police? Wow—she is something special."

I offer the cop a hundred rand for his 'cold drink.'

"I am still thirsty," he says. So I offer another hundred.

"Very thirsty," he says. And I give him yet another hundred. He relents—yet still has the gall to ask for the Bible and rosary. To ask for a blessing. So I'm forced to oblige—handing him the book and beads and laying my hands on his shoulders and murmuring the Lord's Prayer.

"How much did Mum Mary have to pay when she was pulled over?" I ask Themba.

"One hundred rand only," he says.

"I knew it! Trying to screw the tourists. Just like in New York."

Themba's school is just a little further up the road. But because of getting pulled over, we're late. The schoolgrounds consist of nothing more than a row of rectangular cinderblock buildings surrounded by a razor wire fence. A flock of students are gathered outside the entry gate. These kids are late too. A man in a janitorial uniform stands in front of the gate as well—whipping kids with a belt as they enter. "What the hell is going on?" I ask Themba.

"He is punishing them. That is the punishment for being late."

"You can't just beat a kid for being late," I say.

"It is what they do."

"Well I'm not letting that guy touch you."

"Please no. Please no, Victor! You must let me go."

"Why?"

"My friends—if you stop the whipping—my friends—they will tease me," he says. And it clicks. I get it. I'm like the mom who insists on kissing their kids on the lips in front of school while dropping them off.

"Okay. Suit yourself. Get your butt whipped. But just so you know—it's wrong."

Themba proceeds into the flock and greets his friends. Then turns back and whistles for me to look. He takes a textbook from his bag and sticks it down the backside of his pants. When it's his turn to enter the gate, he runs through, and takes a fierce crack across the ass. But then he turns back to the man, sticks out his tongue, and removes the textbook from the pants. The man curses at him and he runs. The crowd of kids cheer. Themba is the hero of the morning.

I'm glad I didn't intervene.

∞

fourteen

I am teaching preschool kids to read. Lazarus, the little boy whose dead mother we carried from her home, is one of my students. I've never taught anyone anything in my entire life—so nevermind trying to teach mewling children with flailing arms and zero body control the nuances and idiosyncrasies of English vowels. But this is Mum Mary's requirement for my room and board, so here I am.

Mum Mary's community center is called Good Hope—a former elementary school complex similar in size to Themba's school—a series of brightly painted rectangular cinderblock buildings spread out over a patch of dirt. Each building provides employment in a different department for the gogos—a woodshop, a bakery, a library, a seedling garden, and this preschool for the orphan children not yet in school.

A small shelf of donated books are my only available teaching materials. I grab the first book I touch: *The Little Blue Bird Who Learned to Fly*. I stand there and read it out loud at first. But the kids don't listen—squirming and squawking and scattering away by the second page. Chaos in the form of five-year-olds crashing into walls and careening off each other like Themba's marbles. I start acting out the story—craning my neck and chirping with a pretend beak as I mime eating a worm from my mother's mouth. This grabs their attention. And then I'm flapping my wings—skittering around the room trying to get away from Mr. Cat. And then finally, I'm jumping off a chair and holding out my wings triumphantly—I rescued my mother, escaped Mr. Cat, and finally learned to fly. The kids clap and cheer. I bow. I'm proud of myself—especially for making Lazarus happy. Now if only I could figure out how to fill the remaining hours of the day. And the rest of the week.

∞

fifteen

The following Saturday I go back into the cane fields with Jabulani and Sabelo. I'm looking for Ayanda. She's been on my mind all week—through endless reenactments of children's books, through temper tantrums and pee-soaked pants, through morning mangos and afternoon marbles with Themba, through mush stew dinners and toothbrushing rituals, through my isolation and loneliness and thoughts of home—all along I've been thinking about her. About her radiance—her pain, her grace, her smile.

A sea of dancing bodies undulates to waves of light and sound. And as I stand behind Jabulani and Sabelo on the DJ platform, King Nkosi pulls up with his entourage in his Range Rover. Again, he's wearing a flashy silver suit and a purple tie. He looks like a swollen big toe. His thugs are dressed more casually in black t-shirts and jeans—but they too flaunt their status with gaudy gold chains and oversized watches. A second car—a black Mercedes sedan—pulls up behind them. A bevy of beautiful woman pour out of it. Ayanda is one of them—dressed again in a flowing yellow dress. I call to her over the music and wave. She flashes a smile then turns away to join the other girls in attending to King.

I wander up onto the hill and sit in the grass under the light post. Close my eyes—the heat of the night radiates around me. I think of Marco—of drinking on his rooftop. I think of Liam—of listening to him play guitar. I wipe sweat from my brow and look up—Ayanda is standing there holding two beers. "Unjani, Victor," she says folding down into the grass beside me and handing me a bottle.

"You remembered my name…"

"Yebo! Do you remember mine?"

"Do I remember it? Ayanda, I haven't stopped thinking about you."

"Yoh! You are too funny. Oogy wawa—cheers," she says and clink bottles.

"Thanks for the beer."

"Pleasure!" and then leans her head on my shoulder.

"What happened?" I ask pointing to her lip—bruised and cracked.

"It is nothing."

"Was it that guy King? I saw him last week."

"I work for King."

"Why don't you stop—working for him?"

Ayanda pulls away from me. Takes a long swig of her beer.

"What? What did I do?" I ask.

"It is easy for you to say. To leave King."

"I just mean that if he hurts you—why do you work for him—you don't have to do what you do—I mean I don't blame you for what you do—money is money—I just mean you could do something else. I could talk to Mum Mary. I bet she could get work for you. I could ask her."

"You are too funny, Victor," she says laying her hand on my cheek.

"Why do you keep saying that?"

"You do not know the troubles of my life."

"You wouldn't believe the troubles I know," I say taking her hand in mine.

"Whatever troubles you think you know—I have known more—too much more."

"That's not true."

"If I do not work for King. I will not eat. I will not live."

"Here take this—I have more," I say handing her all the money in my pocket.

"I don't want this from you," she says pushing my hand back and pushing herself away.

"Did I offend you?"

"I don't want your money."

"Well, what do you want?"

Ayanda smiles. Leans into me. Places her forehead against mine.

"A friend," she says, "I want a friend."

I look at her. "I want to be your friend too."

One of King Nkosi's thugs comes up the hill to fetch her.

"I'm sorry. Sala kahle. I must go," she says and kisses my cheek.

"I need a friend too," I yell as she is dragged away.

A barefoot drunken man approaches me. He swaggers and waves a broken bottle in my face. I'm taken aback—distracted by Ayanda's disappearance into the crowd. "Give me money rich man," the man says.

"Excuse me?"

"Give me money. I saw you have money."

"I'm a priest. A preacher. I have no money."

"I saw you. With the lady. You give her money. You a rich man."

"I'm not. I swear. I have no money."

The guy jabs the broken bottle at my face. "Whoa! Whoa! Here! Here!" I yell turning out my pockets. "Take it. Take it," I say flinging money in his face. I run—and he lunges. He gouges me in the rib. Red hot heat erupts. Blood flows down my side. I trip—tumble down the hill. Get up. Fight through the crowd. Climb up onto the platform. Lift up my shirt. Show Jabulani and Sabelo the wound.

I lay across a wicker bench on Mum Mary's patio. My shirt off— I'm dripping blood. Themba mops the ground. The triplets watch from the shadows. Jabulani and Sabelo compress cloth on the wound. Mum Mary sterilizes forceps and prepares a needle and thread for sutures. She pierces my flesh and begins to stitch. It burns and stings. But there is no pain—only discomfort.

"How'd you learn to do this?" I ask her through a grimace.

"You would be surprised by the skills you learn in service to God."

"So I'm not the first person you've stitched up?"

"If you are the first then you should be concerned."

"Should I be?"

"Shush now! This is but a flesh wound. Concern yourself with salvation."

Mum Mary finishes lacing six tightly woven stitches across my ribs. Jabulani and Sabelo help me to sit upright. Themba fetches me a glass of water. The triplets giggle and point at the wound. I chug the glass of water. I'm woozy—dizzy. But I steady myself—look at Mum Mary. "King Nkosi—why do you work with him?" I ask.

"Yes, yes. Mr. Nkosi. Now—he is a man who creates with ego."

"You didn't answer my question. Why do you work with him?"

"Mr. Nkosi is a very powerful man. An evil man. But God is not a table. I work with him. I accept his money—I take his money—so that justice shall be done. We must combat his evils with faith. If I did not work with him—he would work against us. His day will come—justice will be done. But until that day—I prefer to keep the devil in my garden rather than allow him to ransack my house."

∞

sixteen

The morning heat rises. I lay in bed in a sleepless stupor—groggy. Themba comes into the cabin with a fresh dressing for my stitches. Mangos too. We sit on the stoop and watch the wind blow through the tall grass. Stitch lays at our feet—licks our toes. She can barely walk now. The babies will be coming soon.

"Last night—I saw the scars—on your back," Themba says.

"Yeah. There's lots of them, right?"

"Too much."

"Tell that to my mother."

"Your mother did those to you?"

"Yebo, yes," I say and ruffle Themba's head.

"If my mother would do that to me then I am glad I do not know her."

"Don't worry about that. Don't worry about me. Just be glad you got Mum Mary."

"Mum Mary is a very special lady. I am too much grateful for Mum Mary."

"That's good. You should be."

"I am too much grateful for you, Victor."

"I'm 'four' grateful for you, Themba." And we laugh—and it hurts.

We set out on an adventure. Mum Mary is gone. She has taken the triplets with her to Cape Town for the week on a fundraising mission. So Jabulani, Sabelo, and Themba are taking me on a hike. "You have been sour, bhuti. We are worried about you," Jabulani announces to me on behalf of the others. And it's true. Since that night I got stabbed—I haven't left the compound besides going back and forth to the community center for work. And I've been drinking too much. There were even a few days last week when I started slurring my words while reading to the kindergarten kids. I'm lost again. Liam tells me I need to have faith in myself—in love. And I know he's right. But I'm struggling to find it—my faith. I'm settled here. But so far from home. And with no one—save for a friendship with a ten-year-old and a one-sided infatuation with a prostitute I've spoken to twice. So yes, I've been sour. A hike will do me good.

We are climbing to the top of the highest peak in the green mountains of the Nkomazi. Locally it is referred to as 'Thimble Mountain'—because of its round rocky outcropping at the top. But Themba tells me that the boys at his school call it 'Nipple Mountain'—and rumor has it that there is a whole village of naked woman who live at the top. We follow the path through the tall grass and cane fields, passed a herd of roaming cattle, across a muddy stream, and up into the rolling foothills. It's hot and humid. My shirt is soaked with sweat. And I have to squint to avoid the glare. Jabulani and Sabelo carry gallon water jugs and walk quickly—practically jogging up the trail. I plod along behind them—out of breath. Themba walks by my side. "You don't have to wait for me, you know," I say.

"I know," he says.

"You can run along ahead with them if you want."

"I want to stay with you, Victor."

We reach a plateau. Jabulani and Sabelo grab sticks and hit rocks off the cliff. Themba picks one up too. Throws up a rock and swings. It dribbles forward—barely reaching the edge of the plateau. Jabulani and Sabelo mock and tease him. So I pick up his stick, toss up a rock, and smash it—a long ballooning shot. Themba jumps on me and cheers—tackles me to the ground. Jabulani and Sabelo jump on me as well. Unbridled silliness—we howl and laugh as I'm crushed below the impromptu pig-pile.

We climb for hours. Lush flora gives way to spindly pines. The air smells of sap. Dry needles crack beneath our feet. The day gets hotter. I wheeze from altitude and heat. And our water is nearly gone. But huffing and puffing I scramble up the rocky ledge and reach the peak. Only to be greeted by two soldiers pointing machine guns at us. Let me repeat—two dudes in military fatigues are screaming at us while shoving automatic rifles in our faces.

I pull Themba behind me to shield him and raise my hands. Jabulani and Sabelo step forward with their arms up and address the soldiers. They speak in SiSwati, so I can't understand the conversation. It starts out contentious—but quickly turns jubilant. Jabulani is recanting some kind of comedic monologue and the soldiers are laughing. Sabelo and Themba start to laugh as well. The guards lower their weapons, wave at us, and depart back down the other side of the mountain.

"What was that all about?" I ask.

"They are from the army. They are guarding the border. We are on the border with Swaziland. They are looking for smugglers. Many drugs are carried through these mountains. And they thought we are smugglers. But I told them that you are a volunteer from America—that we were showing you the mountain. That you were eating wild berries. That you have been pooping all over the mountain."

"And they really thought that was funny?"

"Yebo! It is very funny."

"Gee, thanks," I say, "so glad I could help."

We stand atop the rocky thimble looking out over the vastness of the Nkomazi. Rich green and brown brushland. The brindled concrete villages. Crisscrossing furrows of dirt. Blue haze on the horizon. We can see it all from here. We sit and rest and look—chugging the remains of our water. Then lay on our backs and look up at the sky.

"What kind of animal does that look like?" I ask pointing at a cloud.

184

"A dog," Jabulani says.

"No. An impala," Sabelo says.

"I see a donkey," I say.

"No. No. It is a lion!" Themba roars.

"Sho! It is a lion," Sabelo says.

"Yebo! A lion," Jabulani says.

"Well, I guess it's a lion then," I say.

Out of water—we take a short cut down the mountain. Sabelo assures us he knows the way. But we get lost. And find ourselves trudging down a treacherous slope of loose rock and thick briar. Every couple of steps one of us stumbles, twists an ankle, or gets pricked by a thorn. We trample through the brush for over an hour with no signs of a trail. We're thirsty—throats so dry it makes it hurt to swallow. It's too late to turn back now so the only way through is forward. I pick up the pace—exhausted and frustrated—charging headlong into the briar. I trip—fall—roll head-over-heels down the mountain. Then come to a stop face down in the dirt. I roll over, spit dust from my mouth, and groan. I can hear the boys calling and galloping down after me.

"Victor! Are you okay?" Themba says standing over me.

"Yeah. I think so."

"You rolled very far—very fast."

"Like one of your marbles."

"Yebo! Like a big marble!" he says. Jabulani and Sabelo appear over me now too.

"Eish! That was a bad fall," Sabelo says.

"Are you hurt, bhuti?" Jabulani asks kneeling beside me and grimacing at my left arm.

I sit up and examine my elbow. I've got a gash on it. And cuts and scratches all over. But nothing throbs or appears to be broken. So all-in-all I'm okay. The guys help me to my feet. I steady myself on Themba's shoulder. And we hike forward.

We come upon a stream. Holler in excitement—strip down and jump in—splashing and laughing in the cool waters. It's not deep, maybe two feet. The flow is steady—smooth. I reach under and grab a rock. Use it as an anchor and pull myself down—submerge—the scratches and cuts and scars and stitches burn. But then are soothed by the flow. I lose myself—floating—the current drowning out feeling.

When I'm out of air, I come back up—breathe—then go back under.

I'm happy here—back in the womb.

The three guys are drinking from the stream.

"I don't think that's a good idea," I say, "that'll make you sick."

"It is okay to drink," Sabelo says.

"This is the stream that feeds our well," Jabulani adds.

I bend down, cup my hand, sip cautiously. Seems okay.

Then I'm chugging—gulping down water—it's never tasted so good.

A crescent Moon rises into the speckled night. We braai. Fire up the grill and cook a mountain of meat. Sit around the firepit and drink whiskey—a cold bottle of Coke for Themba. We get drunk and full and tell stories about love and heartbreak. Jabulani shares the sorrowful tale of his unrequited passion for Nomvula. Sabelo recounts his saga of having his heart broken by Sizile. I tell them a partially true version of my cruel breakup with Jinhee. And Themba....

"Precious!" Jabulani and Sabelo scream in unison.

"No! No! No!" Themba screams back.

"Who is Precious?" I ask.

"Themba wishes for Precious to be his girlfriend," Sabelo says.

186

"Sho! Themba wishes for Precious to be his wife!" Jabulani yells over him.

"No! No! I do not like her!" Themba pleads and blushes.

"Precious...Precious...Precious!" they chant while making dramatic kissing sounds.

And the harder Themba protests—the harder we laugh.

∞

seventeen

It's late—pitch black.

"Vic-tor…Vic-tor…Vic-tor!" Themba moans.

I struggle to my feet and out onto the porch.

"I do not feel good. I am sick," Themba cries. I sling my arm around him and help him to the bathhouse. But we don't make it in time—and he vomits in the grass. We go in the bathhouse and his body is exorcised. The poor kid poops and pukes until his insides are dry.

I stand by him and try to reassure him. "You're going to be okay," I keep repeating.

Jabulani and Sabelo come barreling into the bathhouse as well. They're sick too.

And soon—I'm also sick. It was the water from the stream. We shouldn't have drank it.

All four of us take turns in the stalls. Our shared sick and stink compound our torture. Themba has it the worst. Even in my nauseous agony I think about him. He is suffering—moaning and gasping—his immunocompromised body convulsing in protest. He writhes and clutches my hand. "You're going to be okay," I say again. But I'm not so sure that's true.

The Matsamo Clinic is a single brick building painted pink. Inside the emergency entrance are three rows of orange plastic chairs and a registration desk that sits behind a grate of iron bars. It's quiet when we enter—only one other patient waiting, an old lady rocking back-and-forth and clutching at her head. Jabulani and Sabelo go up to the metal gate to speak with the receptionist. I carry Themba to the chairs. He sprawls out across two of them and buries his head into my arm. His moans are constant. I hold a plastic bucket in case he has to vomit.

We wait.

And wait.

Themba gets worse and worse and worse.

"He needs an IV immediately," I say to the receptionist.

"He must see the doctor first," she says.

"He's sick. What don't you understand? He needs help now."

"He must see the doctor first," she says again.

"Well where is the doctor? We've been waiting!"

"She is busy."

"Well, when will she not be busy."

"When she has finished surgery."

"And when will that be?"

"When she is finished."

"Well, that's just great!" I say and flip one of the orange chairs across the floor.

"Victor!" Sabelo says. "You must not. She will call the police."

"Call the police," I yell. "But please—call the doctor while you're at it!"

The receptionist gets up from her chair, goes into a back office, and closes the door.

"That is why they put the bars between us," Jabulani says.

Eventually we see the doctor. She appears looking haggard and overworked in a stained white coat. She is young—but has the puffy eyes and bloated face of someone who has not slept in a very long time. She acts nonchalant and speaks in a curt tone. "He is very weak," she says, "I understand that he is HIV positive. His immunocompromised body is reacting poorly to the dirty water you drank. I am going to give him antibiotics and fluids and monitor him overnight."

"Is he going to be alright?" I ask.

"He needs antibiotics and fluids. He needs to be monitored. He is very weak."

"Yes, I heard you. But is he going to be okay?"

"He needs treatment and rest."

"You're not answering my question."

"Excuse me," she says, "I have other patients to see." And she turns and leaves.

Themba stabilizes with medication and fluids. His vomiting and diarrhea stop. But he is weak and pale. Goes in-and-out of consciousness—and painful cramps startle him awake. His room is sterile and bare—white washed walls and concrete floors. A single bed and metal folding chair. There's a small sink too. But no running water.

Jabulani and Sabelo head home with plans to come back in the morning. Mum Mary has been informed. She's scheduled to fly back early tomorrow from Cape Town. I settle into the metal folding chair beside Themba to sit vigil for the night. His skin is hot to the touch, yet at times he shivers cold. He murmurs and howls in the midst of a fever dream. I hold his hand and watch his chest rise and fall. Sorrow jackhammers in my chest. This is dread. A piercing fear drilling through my nervous system. I'm afraid Themba is going to die.

A cockroach climbs along a crack in the wall. Halfway up it forks in three directions. I'm desperate for a sign—desperate for some semblance of control—so I strain and focus and will the roach to stay on the middle path. And it does! Reaching the fork and continuing up the middle crack just like I told it to. It's a symbol of hope. But then the roach veers off the path entirely—heading towards a hole in the ceiling. I take off my right shoe, waddle to the wall, leap, and slap at the roach. But I miss and it escapes into the hole. "Dammit!"

Themba grunts. I turn back. He's awake and staring at me.

"Victor, what are you doing?" he wheezes.

"There was a bug. I tried to squash it. But I missed."

"Oh," he says.

"You go back to sleep now. You need your rest."

"My mouth tastes bad."

"I know, mine too. We threw up a lot."

"Can I have some water?"

"Yeah. Let me help you." He struggles to sit up. Takes a few meager sips of water.

"We didn't brush our teeth," he says.

"Don't worry. We will," I say.

"I do not want to sleep," he says, "I am afraid."

"You've got to try. You need your rest."

"But I do not want to sleep."

"Then you just lay there and relax. I'll be right here."

I wake up to a nurse nudging me on the shoulder with her shoe. I fell asleep on the floor beside the bed. I can feel the imprint of my shirt seam on my face. My cheek is wet with drool. The nurse greets me kindly. And I jump up.

"Good morning, bhuti! You have been snoring very loud. Like a bullfrog," Themba says sitting upright in the hospital bed. He's smiling. His lips are dry and cracked. He still looks pale and weak. But he's awake and smiling—and that's all that matters.

"Can we go home yet?" he asks.

"Soon," I say, "soon."

It will be another three days before Themba is allowed home. The sickness has riddled his already weakened immune system. But he is stable and expected to recover. Even so I spend my days and nights by his side in the clinic. We play marbles and cards for much of the day.

Mum Mary visits—reading the Bible and saying the Rosary. At which point, he pretends to nap so he doesn't have to pray along with her. Jabulani and Sabelo bring the triplets to visit too. They poke and prod at him. He feigns annoyance—but he loves their attention. And for the rest of the time, he sleeps. There are no cots or extra beds available, so I camp out on the floor. I actually sleep better on the cold concrete than in the insulated heat of the wooden cabin.

On the last afternoon Themba tells me to go home. "You are smelling bad, bhuti," he says. And it's true. I stink. And have bad breath. And haven't changed my clothes since we got here. The nurses have been giving Themba sponge baths and fresh gowns. But I've been sweating and stressing and eating nothing but biltong and candy from the neighboring Indian shop.

"Are you sure it's okay?" I ask.

"Yebo! I will be okay."

"Okay. But I will be back first thing in the morning with Mum Mary to take you home."

"You must check on Scratch," he says.

"I will."

"She will be having her puppies soon. You must make sure she is okay."

"I will—I will. I promise."

∞

eighteen

Ayanda leans against my motorcycle outside of the clinic. I stare at her as if she is an illusion.

"Take me for a ride," she says.

"What are you doing here?"

"Your brother told me you were here."

"Liam?"

"Mum Mary's boy—Sabelo."

"Oh. Got it. I suppose he is my brother now too."

"He told me I could find you here."

"You've been looking for me?"

"Yebo, yes. I wish to speak to you."

"About what?"

"Take me for a ride. Then I will tell you."

I hesitate before approaching her. She is dressed casually in a t-shirt, jeans, and sneakers, and yet, still appears glamorous in an array of beaded necklaces, a brightly woven tote, and a golden headwrap. My heart beats fast and I can feel sweat on my brow. But I walk towards her. "I'm sorry, but I smell."

"Excuse me?"

"I haven't washed."

"That is okay. I will hold my breath."

"But really—I stink."

"I have known worse."

"Where do you want to go?"

"I will show you."

I start up the bike. Ayanda slips on behind me. I offer her my helmet, but she refuses. We ride off, and she points out directions. The sun slips below the horizon, and the sky burns orange. She wraps her arms around me. Bliss cascades upon me. But not for long. Because all I think about is my stink. I ride faster to diffuse my odor in the oncoming air. Ayanda clenches her thighs against mine and releases her hands. I turn back. She is flying free—arms wide—her headwrap rippling in the wind.

We turn down a farm road—ripping through dirt as citrus groves blur by us. We come to rest at a reservoir. Thick with lily pads and reeds. Frogs croaking. Locusts humming. Ayanda gets off the bike and wanders to the water's edge. She sits under the bough of a canopy tree. I join her in silence—honoring the tranquility of the moment. She takes a joint from her tote bag and lights it. Takes a long, luxurious puff from it, and passes it to me. I inhale and she leans her head on my shoulder. I close my eyes—begging the universe: may this moment never end.

"This tree is called Marula," she says pointing to the branches above us. "It is sacred in South Africa. We make medicine from its bark. We make ointments from its leaves. We make tools from its wood. We make food and drink from its fruit. And we make love under its branches. All that is needed is grown in the seeds of this tree."

"That's beautiful. What you said—and how you said it."

Ayanda lifts the joint from my hand. Inhales. Watches the smoke. And sings. Soft at first. Whispered cries. Almost like a prayer. Then louder. Smooth and mellifluous. Her song painted in harmonious melody—blue and green and yellow and red. And then a majestic chorus—echoed out in a resplendent crescendo—the stars above us appearing and shimmering in percussive symphony. She sings:

> *"I walk along red dusty roads,*
> *In strange and familiar places,*
> *Where devil shadows hide their load,*
> *On dirt black and fallen faces.*
> *On shoulders poor, weary, and dark,*

From wandering so long alone,
I pray and search for Heaven's mark,
Where I might rest my bones.
And as my life begins to fade,
I hear the hope of Nature's song.
The branches of Marula's shade
They have been calling all along.
There is love under this sacred tree,
Come, come—and lay with me."

"That was incredible," I say.

She shrugs.

"Whose song is that?"

"My song."

"You wrote that?!"

"You do not think I could write a song?"

"No. I didn't say that."

"Just because I am poor does not mean I am stupid."

"I didn't say that either."

"I went to school. I read. I listen. I like to learn."

"I didn't mean it that way."

"I should not have sung."

"Yes. Yes! You should have. That song. Your voice. This moment…"

"What?"

"It is the happiest—the most beautiful…"

"You are too funny, Victor."

"You're incredible—you should be a professional singer."

"That will never happen."

"Why not?"

"You are rich. That is a dream you may have."

"I'm not rich…"

"My dreams must be simple. To live. To eat. Maybe to love."

I don't respond. We finish the joint and watch the sky turn from purple to black.

"What did you want to talk to me about?" I ask her.

"Themba."

"Themba? How do you know Themba?"

"He is my son."

"What?"

"Themba. I know he has been sick. I know that you have been staying with him at the clinic. I know that you have been caring for him. I spoke with Jabulani and Sabelo. After we first met. After we talked the last time. I wanted to go to Mum Mary. I wanted to see my baby. I want him to know that I am his mother. Themba is my son."

"How? Explain."

"I told you. When we met the first time. I gave my baby to Mum Mary. I had him when I was very young. Fourteen. I was raped. By my uncle. I was staying with him. My parents sent me to him from Swaziland. He was drunk and came for me. I ran away. Lived with a gogo. I heard about Mum Mary. That she helps people. That she takes care of orphans. When I had my baby, I took him to her. I wrote her a note. I left him with her. I left my son—Themba."

"I don't know what to say—let's go see him now—I can take you to him."

"No!"

"He would die to see you. To know you. To know you were alive. To know you care."

"No! No! It is too dangerous right now. I work for King right now."

"What's he going to do?"

"He is a very dangerous man. He will not like it."

"But Mum Mary—she can help—she will help."

"Please! I am telling you because I want you to know. I want you to keep him safe."

"I love Themba. Of course I will keep him safe. But he needs to know his mother."

"It is too dangerous."

"Just quit. Tell King you quit. Tell him you're done. I promise—Mum Mary will help."

"It is too dangerous."

"Please. Trust me. Let me help you."

"You must not. Not now. But I promise. I will make a plan. I will leave King. And then I will come for Themba. I will speak with Mum Mary. I will ask for forgiveness. And I will finally know my son," and she wraps her arms around me in a hug. And we stay there huddled together—watching the bright stars shine through the dark night—under the leaves of the Marula Tree.

∞

nineteen

Themba is emaciated when he arrives home. I make no mention of Ayanda. We have to help him walk. He's been ordered on a weeklong bedrest. But he's too excited to lay down. Scratch has gone into labor. And he insists he's present for the birth of the puppies. Mum Mary is hesitant to allow it, but then acquiesces. So I bring my mattress outside beside Scratch's whelping box for Themba. The whelping box—made from timber scraps and filled with old newspaper—sits in the shade of what I now know is a Marula Tree.

"Have you seen her give birth before?" I ask.

"Sho! Many times. Scratch gets pregnant too much."

"Then why are you so excited?"

"Because it is beautiful, bhuti. Have you seen puppies born before?"

"No—actually. I've never even had a dog. We had a cat growing up—Patches."

"You will see, bhuti. It is beautiful. The birth of the puppies. It is so beautiful," he says watching Scratch's every breath—even as he struggles to hold himself up over the whelping box. His excitement is unmatched by the others, however. Mum Mary has disappeared into her house. The triplets are off playing in the garden. And Jabulani and Sabelo are busy with repairs on their car.

Scratch's belly is distended. Her eyes are squinted shut. And she winces as she breathes. The first pup slides out of her looking like a jelly fish. A gush of fluid and blood follows. Scratch starts licking the pup and eating away the membrane. The pup doesn't move at first. Its black fur wet and matted. Then it starts to sniff and crawl towards Scratch's nipples. It latches. More pups come. A whole litter of gibbering puppies flop around in search of milk.

"Well Themba—when you're right, you're right."

"What does that mean?" he asks.

"This is a beautiful thing. Magical. Truly, magical. I've never seen anything like it."

"Yebo! I told you, bhuti. It is too beautiful."

Three hours later, Scratch is writhing in pain. Something is wrong. It's been an hour since she delivered her last pup—the twelfth of the litter. She won't let the puppies feed—keeps clawing them away. Themba pats her belly and she moans. I lift her tail to inspect. She snaps and growls at me. But I catch a glimpse of another pup stuck inside her.

"Quick, Themba," I say, "you need to hold her down, we need to help her." And despite his weakness and fatigue, he crawls on top of Scratch, wraps his hand around her muzzle, and pins her down. I have no idea what I am doing. But something needs to be done. So I lift her tail and reach my hand inside. She snarls and kicks. But I feel it. Grab it. Pull. A thirteenth puppy is born—dead. Limp and wet in my hands.

"Poor thing," I say putting it in the whelping box.

"Shame!" Themba says.

Scratch's relief is immediate. She pants and allows the puppies to latch again.

"Look, Victor—look!"

"Whoa!" The dead puppy is moving. "It's alive! It's alive!" I scream.

"It's alive!" Themba screams louder. And I pick him up and hug him and spin him around in a circle. And we laugh. And he coughs because I squeezed him too hard. We are ecstatic. Because the puppy survived. We saved it. It's alive.

Scratch is too tired to move. So I peel off the membranes. The pup breathes and lets out the faintest cry. It's tiny. Fits in the palm of my hand—a runt. Themba pushes the other puppies aside, and we help it to latch.

"Yoh! This one is a miracle," Themba says.

Themba is already beside the whelping box when I wake up the next morning. The puppies suckle on Scratch—squawking and wrestling—fighting to latch. Themba keeps guard over the miracle runt—ensuring it isn't trounced or starved. I crouch beside them and pay witness—enthralled. Sabelo wanders over and inspects the puppies for the first time. Jabulani arrives with a burlap sack. He begins picking up the pups and placing them in the sack.

"What are you doing?" I ask

"Culling the dogs," Sabelo says—clearing his throat.

"What does that mean?"

"We must drown them before they get too big. We cannot keep them," Jabulani says.

"What? You're going to kill them? They were just born."

"We must do it now or they will suffer more," Sabelo says.

"Scratch gets pregnant before we can take her to the doctor," Jabulani says. "But we cannot keep these puppies. There is no one to take care of them. Others cannot afford to feed them. We cannot care for them. They will grow up and become wild. Attack people. Some will starve. It is cruel to let them live." And then he lifts the miracle runt from the whelping box.

"No! Not this one. This one will live," I say, grabbing the pup from Jabulani's hands.

"Mum Mary will not approve of that," Sabelo says.

"I don't care. It barely survived. It's going to live. You're not killing this dog," I yell and look to Themba, who takes the pup from my hands and rocks it in his arms. It coos. The other puppies squeal and squirm in the sack. Jabulani and Sabelo shrug, twist the sack closed, and walk away.

I watch them do it. I watch them drown the puppies. Themba watches too. Tortured sounds of yelping chokes. The pups splash and writhe as the sack is submerged in a large metal wash basin. Jabulani's face contorts with horrid anguish as he holds the dogs under water. Sabelo's glasses drip with sweat as he anchors the other end of the sack. It doesn't take long—and soon there is silence. Jabulani backs away—starts chewing on his finger nails. Sabelo turns his back to the basin and cleans his glasses. The sack floats—ominously still. And then Themba hands me the miracle runt, and starts pulling the sack from the water.

"What are you doing?" I ask.

"We must bury them," he says.

We all help. Me, Jabulani, and Sabelo. We make Themba sit and watch—he already exerted himself too much. We dig little holes in the red earth under the Marula tree. Scratch watches from her whelping box. The miracle runt feeds greedily without competition.

Later, Themba and I are alone again with Scratch.

"Is it a boy or a girl?" he asks about the miracle runt.

"A girl, I think," I say, inspecting the underbelly.

"She is yellow. Like a lion," Themba says slurring his words with exhaustion.

"How do you say lion in SiSwati?" I ask.

"Libhubesi."

"Wait. What? Say it slowly for me."

"Li-bhu-besi. Li-bhu-besi."

"Lay-buh-bessie? Lee-boo-bessie?" We repeat the word back and forth to each other, but I can't pronounce it right. And even in his weakened state, Themba laughs his wild laugh at this. "How about we just call her Bessie?" I suggest. "B-E-S-S-I-E. That's the name of my father's favorite jazz singer. And it's kind of like the SiSwati word for lion. What do you think of that? What do you think of Bessie?"

"Yebo. I like it," Themba says.

"Bessie it is then!"

We brush our teeth in ritual. Bessie squirms and whimpers in the sink basin. Bafana dangles from the corner of his web. Our ritual now officially moved back to the bathhouse, we make our habitual foaming howls in the mirror. Themba laughs. But I begin to cry. Thinking about the birth and death of those dozen dogs. I turn away to hide my eyes—shove my tooth brush into my throat—and gag. I blame my tears on choking.

"Themba, did you know that we would have to drown the puppies?"

"Yebo. But I had hope that maybe we would not."

"How come you didn't tell me?"

"Because I wished that we would not."

"Me too. Me. Too."

∞

twenty

The Nkomazi Cultural Festival occurs the following week. Held at Tonga Stadium—a patchy multi-field complex with a crumbling brick wall around it—the festival is the most celebrated event of the year. Hordes of vendors with tents and tables line the outskirts selling food and drink and crafts and clothing. Musicians and dancers perform traditional songs and dances on a series of scattered platforms and stages. A cow is being butchered in the corner for the afternoon feast. Caldrons and grills bubble and sizzle with aromas of spice and meat. A main stage has been erected at the far end of the stadium. A tented platform on the side of the stage has been reserved for VIPs and dignitaries. King Nkosi in his flashy silver suit sits front-and-center stuffing his face with chicken. I look for Ayanda in the crowd, but there is no sign of her.

I'm working in the HIV testing tent with Mum Mary. Mum Siphiwe, who usually assists with testing, has fallen ill. So I'm filling in and getting trained as a counselor. This is not something I'd feel comfortable doing under normal circumstances, but Mum Mary is not a woman who takes 'no' for an answer. Besides, if this works out, it may turn into a legitimate paying job. My cash stash hidden in Pap's duffel can only stretch so far.

A steady stream of people come for free testing throughout the day. I wear gloves, rub the patient's index finger with an alcohol swab, use a single-use poker to make a prick, extract a drop of blood, squeeze it onto a test strip, and add two drops of buffer solution. Then wait. One line means negative. Two lines means positive. Mum Mary sits beside me and counsels the patients about their results.

The first kid who tests positive is young—sixteen and scrawny with round hopeful eyes. As his results bleed into permanence on the test strip, adrenaline surges in my mouth and makes it taste like metal. I clear my throat to interrupt Mum Mary who is making polite chatter with the kid to keep him calm while he waits. When she sees the results, she doesn't hesitate. She takes the tester and shows it to the boy.

"You have tested positive for HIV," she says in a stern yet concerned tone.

The kid's eyes bug out and he clutches his throat.

"Do you understand what this means?"

He nods his head.

"Medications may allow you to live a long life. But you must also make changes. You must put your faith in God. Pray. Use condoms. Abstain…" Mum Mary continues on counseling the boy. And the boy turns and looks at me. I stare back holding his gaze—trying to send him strength and courage. But my face probably shows the opposite. I'm afraid for the boy—my heart breaks for the boy—his whole world has been shattered.

One after the other, people come for testing. A staggering twenty-five percent of them test positive. Some are shocked. Some cry. Some get angry. Some sit stone-faced. One man even smiles. Mum Mary maintains her composure through it all. She never wavers in her focus—offering stoic concern and a constant message of health and faith.

Ayanda walks into the tent. She flashes me a smile. I get up to greet her, but she shakes her head and signals for me to stay. She turns to Mum Mary and sits down in front of her. Mum Mary begins explaining the testing procedures.

"I do not need a test. I know already that I am positive."

"Then why have you come here?" Mum Mary asks.

"I wish to speak with you, Mum Mary…" Ayanda says and proceeds with her story.

204

∞

twenty-one

Chaos. One of the public drop toilets at the stadium collapses during the climax of the festival. A young girl is trapped inside—pinned down in a festering pit of feces and urine. Ayanda has just finished her confession with Mum Mary when we get the news.

We rush with the crowd to the cave-in site. I lose track of Ayanda. The collapse is a concave pit of debris. I jump into the assembly trying to dig out the girl. Mum Mary jumps in too. The screams of the girl are piercing. Her pleas—afraid and desperate. She is sinking—drowning in the swill. We claw furiously at concrete. The girl wails—panicked. We strain to lift a portion of collapsed wall. Get it inches off the pile. Then drop it. We try again. Lift it nearly a foot this time, but drop it. The girl chokes and gags down below—her struggle emanating up through the cracks of debris. We try to lift again, but fail—it's futile. We hear the girl struggle. Flap her arms in the muddy waste. And then the sound of muffled cries. And then silence.

The sun sets behind us. Mum Mary drives us home. The windows are down and the air whips around us. Our clothes are filthy. Mum Mary's white habit streaked with blacks and browns. The stains of tragedy and death.

"King Nkosi killed that girl," she says.

"What do you mean?"

"He and his brother—C.C. Nkosi, the Premiere of Mpumalanga —they received government funds to repair those toilets. But they are corrupt. And they embezzled the money. They are responsible for that innocent child's death. King Nkosi killed that girl."

"He's a bad man," I say.

"And Ayanda—she is entangled in his web of illicit prostitution. But as she says, she has left him. And we must help her. We will help her. You must deliver the news to Themba about her. That his mother has returned. And if he is pleased by the news, then you must accompany him for visitation. I will not allow him to visit her without supervision. She must earn our trust. She must earn Themba's trust. But he trusts you. And so you must care for him."

"Absolutely. It would be an honor," I say.

"Honor God. Or else you will follow in the path of King—the devil's path."

"How should I tell Themba about Ayanda—about his mother?"

"Pray. Use discretion. Have faith. God will show you the way."

"So trust my gut?"

"God is not a table."

"I still don't know what that means."

"You do not have to understand. As long as you do not follow in the path of King. I know you have a sordid past. But you are a changed man now. You must pay penance for your sins. You must atone by serving God—by serving the children—by supervising Themba. Men like King—they do not understand God. They worship tables. They worship the devil. They worship their own egos. I worked with King because I believed he could be contained. But I have changed my opinion on the matter. King is a merciless devil. And we must not entitle his throne. He must be thrust from the garden into exodus."

"Are you saying you want him dead?"

"I am saying that King is the serpent in the garden. And that God's will must be done."

∞

twenty-two

We sit under the Marula Tree in the pale light of the full Moon. Themba lays beside the whelping box. He strokes Scratch's belly as Bessie nurses. I sit in the grass beside them—wondering—where do I begin?

"Scratch is a good mother," I say.

"Yebo! She is a great mother," Themba says.

"Do you ever wish you could see your real mother?"

"Very much. I wish to meet her very much."

"What if I told you that I could arrange a meeting with your mother?"

"Then I would like to see her."

"But what if I am serious. If I could arrange it, would you want to meet her?"

"Sho! Serious?"

"Serious—serious. Would you really like to meet her?"

"Very much. Too much."

"Then I'll arrange it."

"She has come back?"

"Yes. And she wants to see you."

"Serious?"

"Yes—very serious."

"Oh Victor—I am very much happy. Too happy."

"You aren't angry?"

"No—I am not angry. Why would I be angry?"

"Because she left you—your mother left you here."

"But she has returned. I always knew she would return."

"That's a lot of faith."

"Oh thank you, Victor. Thank you."

"Don't thank me—I didn't do anything. Thank Mum Mary."

Themba hugs me. And I hug him back. The Moon rises higher and recedes in the sky. We gaze at it—our arms slung around each other. Scratch pants. And Bessie whimpers. A symphony of wildlife serenades us from the darkness.

"The Moon looks like a shooter marble," Themba says.

"Yeah it does. Can you see the man on the Moon?" I say pointing.

"In South Africa we do not see a man. We see a woman carrying firewood," he says.

"Oh yeah—I can kind of see it. She's carrying them on her head?"

"Yebo."

"Oh yeah—then I definitely see her."

"I'd like to go to the Moon with you, bhuti," Themba says.

"Well I'd like to go to the Moon with you buddy."

"And Bessie and Scratch too."

"Sure! Why not. All four of us."

"We must promise to go to the Moon together."

"Okay. Let's make a deal. If either one of us is ever given the chance to travel to the Moon then we must take the other person—and the dogs too. We can't go without each other. You, me, Bessie, and Scratch. Together or not at all. Okay?"

"You promise? You really promise?"

"I promise," I say.

"Okay. Good."

"What about you? Do you promise?"

"I promise, promise," he says.

∞

twenty-three

The monsoons pour down upon us. It rains the whole next week delaying Themba's reunion with Ayanda. We pull the whelping box into the cabin. And Scratch and Bessie sleep with me. The rats do as well—scurrying under the floorboards to seek shelter from the storm. Themba eagerly awaits our visit. And we pass the afternoons with marbles and ruminations about trips to the Moon.

On Sunday the rain stops and the sky clears. The roads are wet and muddy so we borrow Mum Mary's truck for our visit to Ayanda. The Nkomazi is bursting with color. Glistening pools of rusty earth. Brilliant greens shimmering with dew. And a shining crayon-yellow sun. Ayanda lives in a remote village called Mangweni. The directions to her house are based solely on landmarks—turn left at this shop, turn right at this tree. But despite some starts-and-stops and a few wrong turns, we arrive at her house—a one room cinderblock structure with a corrugated roof.

Themba bounces up-and-down on the seat bench. My palms are sweaty. Ayanda comes out and stands in her doorway blocking the glare of the sun with her hand. And when she sees us, she smiles and waves.

"That's her," I say.

"Serious?"

"Serious. Serious," I say. "That's your mother."

He smiles—a beautiful beaming grin that I will never forget—then jumps out of the car and runs to her. Ayanda squats down and they throw their arms around each other. She whispers in his ear. And Themba pulls back and nods. He starts laughing his wild laugh. And Ayanda laughs too. I stay in the truck for a while and watch from a respectful distance.

We sit on Ayanda's modest stone stoop and eat the mangos Themba picked this morning. He spent ten minutes up in that tree. Going from branch to branch, inspecting each fruit—selecting only the choicest mangos for this occasion. As we eat, Themba tells Ayanda about our hike and about getting sick and about the birth of Bessie and about our plans to travel to the Moon. He talks so excitedly he has to gasp for breath between sentences.

"May I come to the Moon with you?" Ayanda asks him.

Themba hesitates—frowns—goes quiet for the first time since arriving. He looks at Ayanda—studies her. Then looks to me. I shrug—the decision is his to make. He turns back to her. Reaches out and takes her hand. "You may come with us to the Moon. But you must promise never to leave me again."

Ayanda starts to cry. She pulls Themba into a deep embrace. "I promise," she says.

The truck is stuck. I parked it in the tall grass thinking it would be better than in the thick red mud of the road. All four tires are fully entrenched. Ayanda sits in the front seat throttling the gas. Themba and I push from behind. But the tires just spin and kick up mud. Ayanda calls out instructions to Themba in SiSwati and he runs off to the neighboring houses. Minutes late we're surrounded by a whole slew of kids. Together we push. And with one big heave—Ayanda floors the gas and the truck zooms forward. Themba—still positioned at the back—flops face down into the mud. The surrounding kids point and laugh. Themba drops his head in embarrassment. So I flop down in the mud beside him. He laughs and I fling mud at him. He flings it back—and then a full-on mud fight breaks out with all the kids. We scream and cheer—firing red goop all around.

Themba is so sopping wet that he has to hold up his pants to keep them from sliding off his skinny waist. Seeing this, Ayanda goes inside her house and returns with a man's belt. She kneels down in the mud in front of Themba and threads the belt around his waist. It's far too big. So she loops it and cinches it tight. Then lays her hands across his shoulders and kisses his forehead. He smiles—big and bright—his cheeks splattered with mud.

∞

twenty-four

I step into the sacristy and Father Chimo hands me the phone.

"The house is sold. The money is sent. You're safe," Liam says.

"Really?"

"Yes, really. I've cleared it all with Noah."

"Do they have any idea I'm here at Mum Mary's?"

"No. But they made it clear—if they ever catch you, you're a dead man."

"Even though you gave them the money?"

"I get the feeling the money was to keep me safe. A payoff to prevent them from using me as a pawn to get you back here. Like I said, you can't ever come back. You're there now. That's your home. And Victor—you're a poor man now. As you know, priests aren't millionaires. And I have Mom's care to pay. I'll keep sending what I can through Mum Mary. The exchange rate will help too. But don't expect much."

"Liam—thank you brother. I owe you everything."

"You owe me nothing. But you owe it to yourself to be better. And you owe it to Themba too. Mum Mary told me how fond he is of you. And about the developments with his mother."

"Yeah. He's a special kid. Have you heard him laugh?"

"It reminds you of Pap, right?"

"Yes! So much!"

"I thought the same thing the first time I heard it."

"It's uncanny."

"Or perhaps it's a sign from God. A message to you—to look after him."

"Maybe—just maybe," I say. "How's Mom?"

"About the same—stable. Listen—take care, Victor. I mean it. Take care of yourself."

"I will. I love you, brother."

"I love you too. If nothing else—I'm glad this mess brought us back together."

"Me too. Do you think you'll ever come and visit?"

"Someday. When we're certain it's safe. We'll take Themba on a trip together."

"To the Moon!"

"The Moon? What?"

"Oh—it's a dream Themba and I talk about—taking a trip to the Moon together."

"Alright," he says, "then count me in and sign me up. To the Moon and back."

∞

twenty-five

Life becomes us—me and Themba and Ayanda and Bessie. I transition to working as an HIV counselor and palliative caregiver fulltime. Mum Mary hires Ayanda to take over for me in the kindergarten. She's a natural—reading and singing to the kids, and keeping them in-line far better than I was ever able to manage. On the weekends, Themba and I ride over and visit with her. Bessie comes too—riding in the rear storage pod.

I'm falling in love with Ayanda. Nothing I'd ever act upon—at least not now. Themba's relationship with her is more important. I'd never come between them. I love him too much. But even so, I fall more in love with her every day. She is as smart as she is beautiful. Her little house is filled with books—the library of a Peace Core worker who donated them to her. We often take turns reading to each other on our visits—helping Themba to sound out the difficult words. But mostly, we laugh and play with Bessie in the shade.

Bessie shocks us. Turns out she is male. What I thought was a bellybutton was actually a little wiener. Whoops—I made no claims to be an expert on canine anatomy. Still, Themba and I agree his name should still be Bessie. It suits him—Bessie Boy, the jazz singing golden lion pup. Bessie Boy who flops around the yard chasing after birds and barking after cows. Bessie Boy who loves to nibble and lick at Ayanda's fingers. Bessie Boy who mouths Themba's marbles and runs away with them in the middle of his games. Bessie Boy who curls up and sleeps in my lap when he's tired. Bessie Boy who becomes the mascot of this ragtag family we have formed. The four of us—together we are love. I've never known such happiness.

twenty-six

Themba's birthday approaches. I want it to be special. I want to celebrate him. To show him how much I care—how much I love him. He's turning eleven—an important birthday to me. On our eleventh birthday Pap woke Liam and me up at dawn. He made us chocolate chip pancakes with whipped cream. And then he took us to the zoo and circus in the same day. Liam wanted to go to the zoo, and I wanted to go to the circus. So he took us to both. Afterwards we ate steak and cake and Pap gave us presents—a new baseball glove for me and a magic set for Liam. We both fell asleep holding our gifts in our arms—Pap singing and playing his guitar and laughing his wild laugh as we drifted off to sleep. A month later, he was dead.

On a hunch, I call Vusi—my artistic taxi driver buddy back in Johannesburg. My instincts prove to be correct, and he is able to connect to me to a glass blower. I ride to-and-from Joburg in a single day to pick them up. A hand-blown set of spiraling galaxy marbles with a custom shooter made to look like the Moon. Flecks of silver and onyx within it—shimmering and glowing like full craters on a clear night.

On the morning of Themba's birthday, I wake him up early with chocolate chip pancakes. And then we borrow the truck and head to Kruger Park. We drive around watching the grazing animals. Then graze ourselves on fast food cheeseburgers. Next, we head to Nelspruit where I've gotten us tickets to a traveling Mongolian circus. We eat peanuts and cotton candy. Watch contortionists and strongmen, tight rope walkers and fire breathers, trapeze artists and creepy clowns—all performing under the spotlights of the tattered striped tent.

Now for the real surprise. We pick up Bessie and head to Ayanda's house. I've borrowed a tent from Father Chimo and planned a camp out for the four of us. Ayanda greets us when we arrive with a cake and a present of her own for Themba—a beaded leather belt perfectly sized for his waist.

The sun begins to set. We set up the tent and build a fire and roast marshmallows. Then I give Themba my present. "Bhuti, I am so happy! I am too happy!" he says as he unwraps the marbles. And when he sees the shooter, he recognizes it immediately. "The Moon! The Moon! It is the Moon!" he shouts. "Thank you, Victor!" he says jumping up to hug me and running off with Bessie to shoot marbles in the dirt.

"Yebo. Thank you, Victor. Thank you for being so kind to him," Ayanda says.

"I deserve zero thanks. I should thank him. He's changed my life."

"I would not have seen him again if it were not for you."

"You've changed my life too," I say leaning in and kissing her on the cheek.

She blushes. I add more wood to the fire. She hands me a beer.

"Oogy Wawa—cheers to our future," she says.

∞

twenty-seven

A great storm comes in the night. Hail and violent winds. We are forced out of the tent into Ayanda's house. We light candles and huddle together and read. Bessie Boy whimpers as thunder and lightning cracks and flashes.

Headlights appear shining in the window.

"What's that?" I ask

"Lightning," Ayanda says.

"No—it's a car." I go to the door and open it. I squint. Two men are charging towards me. "Hey!" I yell into the rain and wind. The men move fast. "Hey! Hey!" I yell stepping out onto the stoop. The men grab me and pull me down into the mud. I hear Ayanda scream. They kick and stomp. I feel my ribs crack. The warmth of blood on my face. They turn me over. Bessie barks and growls. I see the headlights. I recognize them—a Range Rover. Themba cries out. A foot comes down on my face.

"Wake up! Wake up—please!" Ayanda shakes me awake. My head splits. My face throbs. My nose is shattered. I look at Ayanda through swollen eyes. She is badly beaten too—bleeding from her temple.

"What happened?" I groan.

"Themba is hurt! Themba is hurt! Wake up, Victor! I need your help!" The call of Themba's name shoots me through with adrenaline and I stumble to my feet. My vision is blurred, but I turn and see Bessie Boy crying over a body. It's Themba—bruised and bloody and shivering.

"Themba, Themba, Themba," I call. "Are you okay? What happened?"

"Victor," he gasps still clinging to his new marble set.

"You're going to be okay. You have to be okay. I need you to be okay."

Mum Mary meets us at the clinic. Themba is taken away. And she follows. Ayanda and I are held back—a nurse attending to our wounds. As I suspected, my nose is smashed and my ribs are broken. In addition to the gash on her face, Ayanda has a broken arm.

"What happened," I ask her.

"King. He came for me," she says.

"The Range Rover," I whisper.

"After his men beat you, King came for me. Themba ran at him. But he slapped him down and threw him out into the rain. His men beat him. And left him there. I tried to fight. But King is big and fat. And his men blocked the door. He held me down. He tried to kiss me. I spit in his face. And he broke my arm and knocked me out."

Ayanda looks at me with tears that will not fall—her eyes filled with sadness and rage.

"Themba—how long was he out there?"

"I don't know. But it is late. It is very late. He was out there for a long time."

We live in purgatory. Sitting vigil beside Themba. He remains mostly unconscious—feverish and delusional on the rare occasion he awakens. He has cuts and bruises all over. He has pneumonia. His body is rejecting the antiretroviral medications. He is suffering. I stay by his side. Ayanda too. We sleep there. A nurse has arranged an extra bed this time. We sleep in shifts. Mum Mary and Sabelo and Jabulani take turns as well. The triplets visit too.

I've placed the Moon shooter in his palm and he clutches it—never lets it go.

Days pass and nothing changes.

More days pass and Themba gets worse.

I sit watch. Flicking his remaining marbles across the blanket. Holding his hand—hoping.

I wake up. Themba's gone—not in his bed. His blankets tossed aside. IV lines ripped out. I run into the hallway. He's not there either. I go back to the room. The window is open. I see Themba—a flash of him—running into the cane fields behind the clinic. There is no time to waste. Ayanda is still asleep. I jump out the window and run after him.

"Themba! Themba! Wait!" I scream.

Themba stops. Turns to me. His eyes are wild and crazed. He takes off again.

"Themba! Themba! Wait! Stop!" But it's no use. He runs deeper into the cane fields.

I chase after him. But he's erratic—darting and changing directions. Thrashing—unencumbered—through row after row. I follow and call after him. Get near. Dive. Tackle him to the ground. He thrashes—clawing and kicking. He screams—calling out horrid primal moans. I wrap him in my arms and clutch him to my chest.

"Themba! Please! Please stop! Please! It's me. It's Victor. I'm here."

He gives up his fight. Goes limp in my arms. And I release him.

"Themba. It's me. It's Victor," I say again rolling towards him in the dirt.

"Victor?" he moans.

"Yeah. I'm here. I'm here. I'm right here."

His eyes become clear and lucid. "Victor…" he whispers.

"Yes! Yes! It's me. I'm here."

"Victor!" he says and laughs his wild laugh—as wild and joyous and fierce as all the mighty animals of South Africa. He laughs—and I laugh with him. I look up and Pap is there too—laughing and smiling right along with us. The whole world is laughing. The sun and sky and clouds and wind and mountains and fields and earth—they all laugh along with us. The entire universe is laughing—the beginning and the end, the alpha and the omega—echoing out in the waves of Themba's laughter.

The laughter fades. Themba and I are alone again in the morning light. Themba looks at me and smiles. Then lifts his hand and opens it. His shooter marble. "The Moon. To the Moon," he says. I take the marble from his hand and squeeze it. Themba dies.

∞

twenty-eight

I say nothing during the funeral. I feel nothing. I can't—the pain is too great. The church is filled with the entire Good Hope community. The triplets sit around me—surrounding me with love. Jabulani and Sabelo give heartfelt readings. Father Chimo gives a reverent homily. Mum Mary gives a solemn eulogy. And Ayanda sings out a glorious hymn. We all mourn together. I clutch the shooter marble in my hand.

Themba is buried in a beautiful field.

twenty-nine

I sit on the stoop of the cabin with Bessie Boy. A yellow canary pecks at the dirt in front of the bathhouse. It poops and chirps and ruffles its feathers. Bessie Boy barks and charges after it. It takes flight and swoops into the bathhouse. Bessie Boy runs after it. I follow.

The canary is caught in Bafana's web. It struggles—wriggling and squawking. It can't escape—the web is too strong. Bessie Boy barks in frustration. Bafana watches from the corner—waiting. I stick my hand into web and grab the canary. It thrashes at first then calms in my hand. I open my palm and it flies away.

It's time for our ritual. It's time to brush our teeth. Time to brush my teeth. Themba is gone. There is no Themba to brush with me. There is no Themba to eat mangos with me. There is no Themba to pat Bessie Boy with me. There is no Themba to play marbles with me. There is no Themba to laugh with me. There is no Themba. No trips to the moon.

I lay on the cool concrete floor of the bathhouse and cry.

Bessie licks the salt from my face.

I ride down to the plaza and buy a bottle of whiskey. I ride out to the cane fields and drink it. The alcohol drowns my sadness and kindles my rage. Then I go for King. I ride to the fields to confront him. I know where he is tonight—the Spinning Stadium.

I hide my bike in the darkness. I lurk through the cane until I see him—holding court with his henchman and harem in front of his Range Rover. A new girl getting assaulted and belittled on his lap. I don't know what I'm going to do—I don't know what I'm doing here. Watching him—stalking him like a predator.

I wait. It's loud. Music and motors and screeching tires. There are new DJs tonight. Jabulani and Sabelo are at home in mourning— sworn to never go near King ever again. But I am near him. So close I can smell his sweat and noxious cologne.

King takes a final sip of beer then throws his bottle into the field beside me. He tosses the young girl from his lap and moves towards me. I freeze. He walks into the cane and stands beside me. I hold my breath. I think about running. But I hold my ground. He starts taking a piss. This is my chance. I grab his shoulder and swing him around. He looks at me surprised and pees all over my leg. I punch him in the mouth— crack my hand on his cheek. My hand explodes with pain. King shakes off the blow and tackles me to the ground. Starts pounding on me. I see the glint of metal in the glare of the stadium lights—then feel the red-hot burning pain of his blade plunging into my shoulder. I scream. Then pull his head down, bite his ear, and rip it off. He releases me and screams now too. I hear the commotion of his thugs coming towards us. I scramble to my feet and spit out his ear. I pull the blade from my shoulder and King charges forward. I stab him directly in the throat. He moans and gags and collapses. I gallop off just as his goons come running through the brush.

I circle back to my bike dripping in blood. My shoulder is gashed. My hand broken. I'm drunk. Adrenaline is surging. I can't feel anything. I race back home swerving and leaking blood across the pavement. Bessie Boy comes barking at me when I reach the gate. I struggle to open it, then ride straight to Mum Mary's house.

"I went for King," I tell her.

"What happened?"

"I stabbed him."

She yells for Jabulani and Sabelo and they come running. She calls out commands to them in SiSwati and then fetches her first aid kit. The triplets appear too—frightened by the oozing blood. Mum Mary scolds them back to bed. And for a second time—she stitches my wounds. "I think I killed him," I say to her.

"An eye for an eye. God is not a table," she says.

Sabelo appears with Pap's duffel bag—packed and filled.

"The money," I say to him.

"It's in there," he says.

Jabulani pulls the truck up to Mum Mary's porch. The back is loaded with supplies. The boys grab me and carry me to the truck. They help me climb into the back and then cover me with blankets. "No! Wait!" I yell. I climb upright and call for Bessie Boy. He comes running. "I'm not leaving without him," I say. No one objects. And he jumps into the back of the truck with me. Jabulani and Sabelo cover me again with the blankets.

"Go well. Be well," they say. And Mum Mary drives us away.

We halt at the border to Mozambique. Mum Mary speaks with the border guards in Portuguese. I hear them walking around the truck—inspecting it. Bessie boy barks. I hear the guards come toward us. Mum Mary's usual calm stern tone changes. There is a lilt of panic in her voice. The truck door opens. Mum Mary's voice grows nearer. She pulls Pap's duffel away from my feet and out of the truck. I hear the zipper open. She's giving them my cash. She's bribing them. And it works. We cross the border and drive through the night.

thirty

I live in Mozambique now. I work at an orphanage run by Mum Mary's first adopted child. I write to Ayanda and Liam often—sending letters through Mum Mary's network of gogos and volunteers. King Nkosi is dead. His fat bulbous body haunts my dreams. But I have no regrets. God is not a table—an eye for an eye. But there is no justice in his death. Themba is still gone. Ayanda still weeps. And we all still mourn.

The past is a misty dream. I wanted to be famous. Now—I just want to love everyone and tell the truth. It may be impossible. But I'm going to try. Because that's all I have now. No Themba. Pap is long gone. Mom is disintegrating. Marco is gone too. Jinhee has forgotten me. Bobby and the bars and streets of New York are mere glimmers in the rearview mirror of a taxi cab. Boris is dead and buried who knows where. The threat of Noah is always lurking. Liam is worlds away in a sacred cathedral. And Bessie Boy lays at my feet as I write this. As I write this to you—hoping like the books of my youth—that this story will reach out and embrace you. That you will carry Themba forward. Make him immortal. Place him among the stars. Think of him every time you look at the moon.

A little girl—Marta—comes running up to me. She is crying.

"What's wrong?" I ask.

The wheel has fallen off her toy car. A car made from wire hangers and elastic bands. It's just like the one Themba and Lazarus were rolling through the dirt the day Lazarus's mother died. I take the car from Marta and inspect it. The axel band needs fixing. It's come untwined. I twist the elastic and fasten it to the wire wheel.

"Good as new," I say handing the car back to her.

"Thank you," she says and runs off laughing.

I think about Themba all the time. I carry his shooter marble around with me everywhere. I will love him—always. Bessie and I take walks at night and contemplate the Moon. One memory above all else stays with me—one of our many times laying out in the grass together with Bessie Boy under the shade of the Marula Tree. I pick Themba up and spin him off the ground like a helicopter—holding him by the wrist and ankle and soaring him through the air. Turning faster and faster—he laughs harder and harder. Bessie Boy runs circles around us—yipping joyously.

"To the Moon…send me to the Moon…fly me to the Moon," Themba yells.

"10…9…" I start a launch countdown as we whirl around-and-around.

"To the Moon…to the Moon…"

"8…7…6…"

"Fly me to the Moon…"

"5…4…"

"To the Moon!"

"3…2…1…lift off!" I yell raising my arms and lifting Themba even higher—pretending that I'm really going to let him go. He screams—ecstatic. I slow our spin and lay him back down in the grass. I fall to the ground from dizziness. Bessie pounces on us—racing back-and-forth to lick our faces. Themba crawls on top of me. He hugs me and presses his ear to my pounding chest. I throw my arms around him and he squeezes me tight. And we laugh.

The End

Acknowledgments

To my wife Lea—this book would not exist without you. Thank you for your restless enthusiasm—for the painstaking hours you spent editing this text. Thank you for being my friend, wife, and partner. Thank you for being an amazing mother to Etta. I love you.

To my mischievous soul brother Corey—this book would not exist without you either. You read and supported every iteration of this story. You believed in me even when I didn't believe in myself. Thank you for being a beautiful, magical, and loving friend.

To Jesse—your cover-art painting is beautiful. Thank you for lending your artistry and talent to this story. Thank you too for your notes. And of course—for your brotherhood and friendship.

To Viral—thank you for the daily support—for believing in the ARC.

To Mike—for your sage counsel—and always having my back.

To the friends and family who provided valuable notes—Matt, Shvarts, Collin, Pat, John, Dave, Linda, Kim, Will, Evan, Lauren, Farrell, Brooke, Brian, Tandy, Anya, and Catriona. And to the friends who supported me along the way—Yerin, Tomo, Changah, Drew, Ryan, Megan, Chloe, Perez, Amy, Dan, Dave, Ben, Gerald, Bill, Mort, and the whole CrossFit Station Crew.

To my extended Judson, Carroll, Valliere family—thank you—it is the blood that binds.

To my brother Phillip—for always looking out for me. I love you.

To my mother and father—for being the best parents and grandparents. I love you.

And finally—this book is dedicated to my two favorite Rays: Raymond and Etta Rae. Raymond—I'm so very blessed to call you bhuti. You are my daughter's namesake. And Etta Rae—you are the greatest thing that has ever happened to me. I will work until my dying breath to make this world a better place for you—and all kids like you. I love you both.